Requests for information should be addressed to:
Zondervan Publishing House
Grand Rapids, Michigan 49530

Library of Congress Cataloging-in-Publication Data

Herndon, Ernest.
    The secret of Lizard Island / Ernest Herndon.
        p.   cm.
    Summary: When a computer error causes the CIA to select twelve-
year-old Eric as an agent for their new wildlife conservation
branch, he finds himself spying on renegade scientists who are
tampering with the monitor lizards on a Pacific island.
    ISBN 0-310-38251-3 (paper)
    [1. Adventures and adventurers—Fiction. 2. Monitor lizards—
Fiction. 3. Wildlife conservation—Fiction.] I. Title.
PZ7.H43185Se 1994
Fic—dc20   93-5011
                                                        CIP
                                                        AC

Edited by Dave Lambert
Cover design by Jim Connelly
Cover illustration by Jim Connelly
Internal Illustrations by Craig Wilson, The Comark Group

Printed in the United States of America

93 94 95 96 97 / LP / 10 9 8 7 6 5 4 3 2 1

For Andy

1

I looked up at the clock on the classroom wall. An hour till the final bell. Sigh.

Suddenly the loudspeaker on the wall above Mrs. Poodlum's desk crackled.

"Mrs. Poodlum!" said a female voice. "Would you please send Eric Sterling to the principal's office?"

"I didn't do anything!" I protested, and everybody around me giggled.

But Mrs. Poodlum just smiled. "You may go, Eric," she said. For a maddeningly strict teacher, Mrs. Poodlum could sure be sweet sometimes.

I slunk out of the room and down the halls, wondering what I had done. Was it the rubber snake I'd put in Sherry's desk? Or maybe the wrestling match with Mark and Jeff when Mrs. Poodlum stepped out?

I opened the main office door and poked my head in cautiously.

"Eric?" Mrs. Fielder said. "Go right in. Mr. Johnson will see you."

"Yes, ma'am."

I went into The Office.

Mr. Johnson sat behind his big desk. You can tell what kind of guy Mr. Johnson is by looking around his office; he's got an autographed picture of General Patton on his wall and a plaque on his desk that says, "The answer is NO." But right away I got my first surprise: Instead of his usual stern look, he smiled! Very strange. The second surprise was the tall, skinny, bald guy in the black suit who sat across from Mr. Johnson.

"Eric, come right in!" Mr. Johnson said, jumping up and shaking my hand—another surprise. "This is Mr. Colson—" he lowered his voice to a whisper—"from the United States government."

The *United States government?* Oh, *great!* I was really in trouble now!

Mr. Colson did not smile; Mr. Colson did not stand. He extended a hand for me to shake. It felt like a dead fish.

"So you're Eric Sterling," he said, cocking an eyebrow. He nodded to Mr. Johnson. "That will be all, Johnson."

"Yes, sir," said our mighty principal, and tiptoed out of the room, closing the door quietly behind him.

Mr. Colson had a narrow, hawk-beak nose and a pinched face. He had a gold watch chain hanging from his vest, and he smelled like after-shave lotion. I had the feeling I'd seen him in old horror movies before, where he'd played either a homicidal butler or an undertaker. He glanced from an open folder in his lap to me.

"So you're Eric Sterling," he said again, and didn't seem at all happy about it. His voice was deep, but it reminded me of the way my voice sounds when I hold my nose shut.

"Uh—what—" I cleared my throat and started over. "Uh—what did I do, sir?"

He glared. "What do you mean, what did you do?"

I shrugged. "I mean, I'm in trouble, aren't I?"

His eyebrows arched again. "Trouble? I should say not—not yet, anyway. Come here. Hold out your arm. Now make a muscle." He squeezed my bicep. "Hmm. I thought it would be bigger."

He looked at his papers and back at me one more time, shaking his head. "Well, you don't look as I expected you to look, Eric, but you're the right boy, I'm sure." He fixed me with a harsh stare. "We never make mistakes," he said, like a snake hissing.

He seemed to be waiting for me to say something. "N-no sir," I finally agreed. "I'm sure you don't."

He nodded slowly, as if I'd said the right thing. Then he stood and stalked to the window, peering out at the playground where happy second-graders ran and shouted and laughed without a care in the world while I sat in here with Dr. Death.

"Ever heard of the CIA, Eric?"

"Sure. Central Intelligence Agency."

"What about WSI? Heard of that?"

"Uh—no sir, guess I haven't."

He laughed grimly and faced me. "Of course you haven't. WSI is one of the newest and most secret branches of the CIA. It stands for Wildlife Special Investigations. Ever since the fall of the Soviet Union and the end of communism in Europe, we at the CIA have been able to devote our attention to other problems. Environmental crime in general, and wildlife crime in particular, are among the biggest of those problems, world-wide. So we formed WSI to stop poachers, to protect endangered species—in a word, to see to it that wildlife laws are obeyed the world over."

"Wow," I breathed. Pretty impressive stuff. But why was he telling me all this if it was so secret?

He sat down at Mr. Johnson's desk. I didn't think anyone but Mr. Johnson did that! Playing with a pencil, Mr. Colson said, "From now on, Eric, you work for WSI."

My mouth dropped open.

"Of course, I know how honored you must feel," he said. "And personally—"

"I'm working for *who*?" I gasped.

"Don't interrupt, please," he said coldly. "Personally, I wouldn't have picked you." He surveyed me disapprovingly. "But our multimillion-dollar computer picked you out of all the boys in the eastern part of the U.S., considering intelligence, character, resourcefulness, and strength." He looked at my biceps one more time. Then, as if to reassure himself, he said, "Our computer never makes a mistake. According to my files," he tapped his folder, "you should be perfectly suited for the job of boy secret agent. In fact, I suppose it's all to the good that you don't look like an agent. Maybe the criminals won't be as suspicious. So! Do you have any questions?"

Questions! I had a *thousand* questions! But I was so stunned I couldn't get my mouth open. Or, more truthfully, I couldn't get it closed.

"Good. I like a boy who doesn't ask questions. Raise your right hand, then, and repeat after me."

Automatically, I obeyed.

"I, Eric Sterling," he began, and I somehow managed to get my mouth closed and then repeated each word, "do hereby solemnly promise that I will risk my life and do whatever is asked of me in the service of WSI."

I couldn't believe what I had just said!

9

"Tomorrow, bright and early, a driver will bring you to my office for your first assignment," Mr. Colson said. He stood. "I believe we're finished here."

"B-but sir, what about school?" I asked, totally confused.

"School? Ah, yes, school. Don't worry about school, Eric."

Wow! Maybe this isn't so bad after all, I thought.

Then he added, "You can make it all up later."

My heart sank.

I turned to go, and as I walked out the door Mr. Johnson and Mrs. Fielder smiled and bowed slightly as I walked by. Mr. Johnson patted my back. "I always said you would go far, Eric," he whispered.

That's funny. That isn't what he said a week ago when he gave me four hours of detention for dropping jello down Lucy Smith's back in the lunchroom.

I walked back to Mrs. Poodlum's room, my mind spinning. Eric Sterling—secret agent?

2

After school I pedaled as fast as I could to Harvey Blast's house. I knocked on the door.

"Why, hello, Eric," Mrs. Blast smiled.

"Is Harvey home?"

She rolled her eyes and pulled the door open for me. "You know the answer to that, Eric. Harvey's *always* home. Since the day he graduated from high school, I can't get him to leave the house."

I stepped from the glaringly bright afternoon into the cool, comfortable dimness of Harvey's house. "That's because he's studying to be the greatest computer genius of all time," I said, repeating the exact words I had heard Harvey use.

"Well, I think he'll make it, as much time as he spends in front of that computer." She opened the door that led to Harvey's basement room, and I hurried down.

Harvey's room was lit only by the flickering green light of his computer screen. My eighteen-year-old neighbor was staring into it, studying tables of numbers. He munched on a cupcake, spilling crumbs down his shirt front.

"Hey, Harv!" I said, dumping my books on a table.

"Shhh!" he said, deep in thought.

I stood still, watching him gaze at the computer. Like his mother had said, Harvey almost never went outside, and when he did his black skin had a sort of greenish tint. I figured it was from so many hours in front of the screen. His eyes were usually bloodshot from staring so much.

At last he punched a key; with a bleep, the numbers disappeared. He swiveled around in his chair and switched on a dim lamp.

"Oh, it's you. Whuzz happenin', kid?"

"Boy, have I got a problem for you!" I said.

"Good. I like problems."

I told him everything, right from the start. "And this Colson guy told me I was perfectly suited for the job of wildlife agent—more than any other boy in the eastern half of the U.S.! Harv, I *know* that can't be true."

"Ain't *that* the truth. All right, let's see. WSI, you say?"

I nodded. "Hey, I hope it's all right that I told

you," I said, suddenly remembering how top-secret it all was.

"Your secret's safe with me, bro," he said, and began rapidly tapping on his keyboard. "Let's see, WSI, WSI—here's one. Wonder Soap International? *That's* not it. How about this one, Wonky Skateboards Incorporated? Nope. There's nothin' on no Wildlife whatever."

"Maybe under CIA—"

"I think I'll look under CIA. Yessir, Central Intelligence Agency. See this blinking light? Means all their files are top secret. So there's a special code to keep anyone from tapping into their central computer banks. This is a tough one."

But he grinned as his fingers rattled the keys.

"There, got it! Thirty seconds. Not bad, huh? You're dealing with the greatest computer genius of all time, you know."

"I know," I said. Who could doubt it?

"Course, this just got us access to department listings. We're a long way from home. Here we go, Wildlife Special Investigations. Uh-oh, this one really *is* top-secret."

He frowned as he punched in codes. Each time the machine made a beeping noise. "*Dang!*" he said in frustration. "I can't break into it. They got it locked up tight, and I do mean tight!" He rapped his fingers on the desktop, lost in thought. "All right, got to think logically," he mumbled. "The CIA's a federal agency. WSI is a new branch specializing in wildlife. Maybe they've got a link-up with some other federal agency. I'll just call up the directory here. Nothing under W's. Hmmmm. Hey, this looks interesting—U.S. Fish and Wildlife Service. Let's see what they got to offer."

A list of names and numbers appeared on the screen. Harvey scrolled through, examining them swiftly. "Okay, look here—they have their own special investigations department. Wonder if there's a connection." He punched a button; the machine beeped, seemed to stall, then displayed a new list of names. Harvey smiled. "This is called goin' in through the back door, Eric. I realize you don't know computers and you ain't no genius, but what I did, see, I took a guess that maybe the Fish and Wildlife Service helped the CIA get this WSI underway. If so, they probably shared the same files, and government being what it is, they haven't gotten around to closing the old ones yet. Understand? Well, anyway, we're in now, boy."

"What's it all mean?" I asked, feeling creepy that he had tapped into top-secret computer banks.

"Let's see if I can find your file." He tapped in a few more commands; the screen changed. "Here it is: Erik Stirling. Well, there's no mistake, pal. You been picked, all right."

"They goofed," I said. "That's not how I spell my name."

"What?"

"I spell my name E-r-i-c S-t-e-r-l-i-n-g."

"Probably just some lazy government typist—"

"Hey, look! That's not my address! That says *Bower* Lane, and I live on *Flower* Lane."

"Whoa! Two mistakes is two too many," he said. "Is your birth date right?"

"No! That lists me as *thirteen*. I'm only twelve."

"Stranger and stranger, my man. But my nimble brain has grasped a possible explanation. I think they've confused you with another Eric Sterling, who spells his name Erik Stirling. Everything lines up, but it's all just a little bit off. Listen. What's your mother's name?"

"Merry. M-e-r-r-y."

"His is Mary, M-a-r-y. And your dad?"

"Rob."

"His is Bob."

"Harv, this is crazy!"

"I'll say. Uh-oh, now we're getting down to the details. And here the similarity ends. This kid is a black belt in karate, a straight-A student, an expert in several subjects, and speaks three different languages. No wonder they want him for a secret agent!"

"But they got me," I said glumly, "a bench-warmer for the baseball team, an expert in getting punished, I'm lucky if I get a C-plus, and I can barely speak one language." I hung my head.

"Cheer up, bro," Harv said, punching me lightly on the shoulder. "You're just a late bloomer."

"I guess."

"Anyway, you'd better straighten out this mistake pretty quick—or you might not live long enough to bloom."

3

After supper that night, I hopped on my bike and pedaled over to the shopping center, where the karate school was. Harv and I had agreed that the first thing I should do was tell the real Erik Stirling what had happened. Then Erik and I could go together to Mr. Colson to explain things and get me off the hook. I just kept remembering Mr. Colson saying, "We never make mistakes." Well, he'd made a beauty this time.

I parked my bike around the corner in an alley. I locked it to a bike stand; there'd been some thefts around the shopping center lately. Then I headed for the door. I figured if this guy was a black belt, he had to study someplace, and this was the closest karate studio.

About twenty kids, both girls and boys, were standing in four rows facing a mirror-covered wall. A man wearing a loose white outfit with a black belt walked among them, shouting commands as they punched and kicked the air.

I sat against the wall and watched. The students wore belts in different colors: white, yellow, green, brown, and red. One boy about my age wore a black belt. The room hissed with the swish and snap of their movements.

The instructor clapped his hands. "All right. Everybody take a seat against the wall." I suddenly found myself in the midst of a group of panting, sweating students who plopped down around me.

"Erik is going to demonstrate a breaking technique," the teacher said, gesturing to the boy with the black belt. Picking up a couple of square boards from a stack in the corner, the instructor pressed them together and held them out firmly. "Let's see a front kick."

The boy stared fiercely at the boards. He was bigger than I am—taller and thicker both—with brown hair and tan skin, and he seemed to be made of solid muscle. He looked tougher than anyone I had ever seen. Suddenly he shouted so loudly that I jumped. So quickly that I could hardly see what he was doing, he kicked the boards with one foot, snapping them in half.

The students around me clapped.

"Is that Erik Stirling?" I asked a girl beside me.

She nodded. "He won the state karate championship this year for boys. Our instructor wants him to go to the nationals."

I gulped.

"Everybody up!" the teacher commanded. "Pair off for self-defense training!"

Erik faced a boy wearing a red belt. When the teacher barked an order, the boy grabbed Erik by the lapels. In an instant, the boy was lying on his back on the floor, and Erik was standing over him, fists clenched.

I shivered. *This* was Erik Stirling? If I talked to this guy, he'd probably break me in two like one of those boards. Not me, man. I hated to admit it, but I was too chicken even to approach him. I was so ashamed, I could feel myself turning red. I got up and walked out.

Some secret agent.

Then, just when I thought I couldn't possibly feel any worse, I rounded the corner into the alley and saw three teenagers trying to break the lock on my bike!

"Hey!" I shouted—then wished I hadn't.

They didn't run. Instead they wheeled, facing me. One pulled out something that greatly resembled a knife.

I backed away. The boys took a step toward me, and I turned to run. "Stop him!" one of them hissed.

They were a lot faster than I was. Before I'd taken two steps, one of them grabbed my collar and shoved me to the pavement. I'd never been so scared in my life! I twisted around and raised an arm, trying to protect myself. But just as the closest bike thief was about to jump on me, the air exploded with a shout. A blurred white figure hurtled through the air, straight at us. Erik! He knocked the boy away from me with a mighty flying kick, then attacked the other two like a human propeller, whirling, spinning, kicking, and punching.

I struggled to my feet, planning to run for help. But I looked over my shoulder at the fight as I lurched away, and my foot caught on something. I tried to reach out with my arms to brace myself as I fell, but my head hit a lamppost—and everything went black.

4

After what seemed like a long, confusing dream, I opened my eyes. A beautiful girl was leaning over me with a caring smile, her sparkling eyes peering into mine.

Was this an angel? Had I died and gone to heaven?

Suddenly her shoulder-length golden hair rustled and parted, and from around her neck appeared the head of a huge snake!

I gasped. This wasn't heaven, so it must be—

"Wait! Wait! It's all right," a boy's voice said. "It won't hurt you."

I sat up and found myself on a bed. Erik Stirling sat in a chair, and the girl—not an angel but a real, live girl about my age—perched on a stool. But there really and truly was a snake coiled around her neck, and I jumped back.

She laughed. "It's just a pet," she said. "This is Fred the python. Say hello, Fred."

The snake stuck out its tongue and wiggled it at me.

"Won't he bite?" I asked.

"Fred would never be that rude to company," she replied.

"Who are you?" I asked her.

"That's what we want to ask you," Erik said.

You won't believe me when I tell you, I thought. Trying to come up with a good way to explain, I glanced around the room—Erik's room, judging from the trophies on the bookshelves and the karate posters on the walls.

"I'm Sharon Stirling," said the girl. "This is my big brother Erik. He brought you home from the alley where you were attacked."

"Do you remember any of it?" Erik asked me.

I nodded. "I remember everything up until when I tripped." I rubbed my head. "Ouch!"

"Here," Sharon said, dabbing my hurt with a cool, damp cloth. "You have a little bump, but it'll get better."

"Now, tell us who you are," Erik said.

"I'm Eric Sterling," I replied.

They glanced at each other. Erik smiled and shook his head.

"No, really, I *am* Eric Sterling," I repeated.

"Wait," Erik said, chuckling. "*I'm* Erik Stirling. You still must be groggy from that bump on your head."

"I promise you, my name is Eric Sterling," I insisted. "I live over on Flower Lane."

Erik laughed. "This is a joke, right? This is *Bower* Lane, not Flower Lane."

I sighed. "It's a long story, and you probably won't believe it anyway."

Just then a woman with short brown hair and twinkly eyes poked her head in the door. "How is our patient?" she asked.

"Doing much better, Mom," Sharon said.

The woman stepped in, followed by a tall, black-haired man whose shadowed cheeks looked like he could grow a heavy beard if he tried.

"We were worried about you for a while there," Mrs. Stirling said.

The man sat on the edge of the bed, took my wrist, and glanced at his watch. After a minute he nodded, then gently probed my head. "No harm done," he said in a deep, quiet voice.

Suddenly, without warning, the most unbelievably loud roaring sound came from outside the window—exactly the kind of sound you'd expect to hear in the jungle. Instinctively I flinched. Erik and Sharon laughed.

"Dad, can we show him the clinic?" Sharon asked.

"Sure. But don't be too long. We need to get this young man home."

My head throbbed when I stood, so I walked slowly. Erik and Sharon led me down a hall and out the back door into the night. A bright patio light burned, shining on a long concrete building behind their house.

"Is that the clinic?" I said, still nervous after that awful roar. "What kind of clinic is it? Is your dad a doctor?"

"Shhh," Sharon said, opening the door. "Come on in."

"Just don't make any sudden movements," Erik whispered.

Don't make any sudden movements? What did he mean by *that*? Warily, I entered the shed, which was totally dark. A strong, musky odor filled my nostrils. Erik closed the door behind us, and Sharon turned on the light.

"May I introduce you to Leo the lion?" she said, gesturing to a huge lion on a chain at the far end of the room.

5

Staring at us sleepily, the lion began to rumble—
as loudly, it seemed to me, as the motor of an
eighteen-wheel truck.

"Why is it making that sound? Is it going to
attack?" I asked, wondering if the chain would
hold it.

Sharon chuckled. "He's purring, silly." She
walked confidently right up to the lion, who began
to lick her.

"Go on," her brother said to me. "Go pet it."

He shoved me gently forward until I was
standing next to the lion. Cautiously, I reached out
and placed my hand softly on its thick, coarse
mane. The animal leaned forward; I tried to lean
away, but he licked my face with a massive

tongue. I giggled. The tongue felt hot and scratchy, like wet sandpaper.

"Look, Leo likes him," Sharon said to her brother.

A chattering noise overhead distracted me. Glancing up, I saw a small monkey hanging from a rafter staring straight down at me! And all around the room, I noticed now, were cages and pens containing all sorts of creatures: a weasel, a fox, a raccoon, lizards, brightly colored birds.

"Here, Fred, it's time for you to go to bed," Sharon said, sliding the big snake into a glass box. It wiggled its tongue at her. "You too, Leo. Come on." She stroked the lion's belly and pushed on it gently until it rolled over into a bed of straw.

"We need to go," Sharon whispered to us. "My animals need their sleep."

"*Your* animals?" I said.

"We'll tell you about it back in my room," Erik said, and Sharon turned out the light behind us.

In his room again, we all sat down.

"How can all those animals belong to you?" I asked Sharon.

"Well, they don't, really," she replied. "Our dad is a veterinarian. He takes care of the animals in the city zoo, and sometimes he brings some of them here to get well."

"Sharon's going to be a vet when she grows up," Erik said proudly.

She smiled. "Dad's teaching me to take care of the animals."

"She's got a special talent," Erik said. "She can talk to animals and it's like they understand."

"Erik," she protested, embarrassed.

"She really can!" he insisted.

"But tell us now who you are—if you're feeling better," Sharon said to me.

I sighed. "Okay, but you have to promise to listen from start to finish without interrupting."

They promised. I told them about being called to the office and meeting Mr. Colson. "And when he told me his computer had picked *me* to be a secret agent, out of half the boys in the country, I knew there had to be a mistake."

"Why?" Erik said.

I snorted. "Why? Just look at me! Do I look like a secret agent to you?"

Erik shrugged. "What does a secret agent look like, anyway?" His eyes brightened. "Hey— maybe it's *better* that you don't look like one. That way the crooks won't suspect—"

"I know, I know," I said, shaking my head. "Mr. Colson said the same thing. But it's not just how I look. Secret agents are tough, you know? And smart, and—well, anyway, I told my friend about it, who's a computer genius, and he tapped into the government's files to find out—"

"Is that legal?" Sharon asked with a frown.

"I don't know, but guess what we found out."

"What?"

"There are two Eric Sterlings in the city. One spells his name E-r-i-c S-t-e-r-l-i-n-g, and the other spells his E-r-i-k S-t-i-r-l-i-n-g."

Their eyes widened as the truth dawned on them.

"You're the one they wanted," I said to Erik.

"Me!"

"This is unbelievable," said Sharon—adding quickly, "but I believe you."

"That's why I went to the karate school, to tell you," I went on. "But after I saw you break that board, I, uh—"

But he was no longer listening. "This is crazy! I don't want to be a secret agent. I'm practicing for the next karate tournament. That and school take up all my time. I don't have time to be a spy!"

"You would be a good one, Erik," Sharon said to him.

"*You* should be the wildlife agent, Sharon," he countered. "You're the one who's an animal expert."

"Well, *I* sure can't be one," I said. "They'll expect me to know karate and all that."

"That's true," Erik said. "You'll just have to tell them the truth. But when they come to me, I'll tell them I can't be a secret agent!"

"Are you sure, Erik?" I asked.

"Yes, Eric, I'm sure," he replied.

Sharon giggled. "Wait a minute! I'm getting

29

confused by all these 'Erics.' I've got an idea. Eric, we'll call you Eric C., and Erik, we'll call you Erik K. How's that?"

"Yeah!" Erik K. said. "The K stands for karate, and the C for—"

"Clumsy," I said, rubbing my head.

6

Dr. Stirling phoned ahead and told my parents what had happened in the alley. When I got home, they fussed over me for a while before I went to bed, even though I assured them I was all right. Parents.

In the morning, I expected to find a car waiting for me in front of my house, as Mr. Colson had said. When no car showed up, I pedaled to school as usual.

Just as I parked my bike, a black car pulled up. The driver, who wore sunglasses, nodded once. I got into the back seat and we drove away.

"Hi," I said. "I guess you're from WSI."

He didn't answer. I sure hoped this was the right car!

We drove into the heart of the city, to a big skyscraper. The driver parked in a covered parking lot, led me to an elevator, put me inside, punched the button for the thirtieth floor, and left. Not a word.

My stomach fluttered as the elevator rose and rose. Finally it stopped, and the doors slid open.

I wandered down empty halls until I found a door with a small sign reading, simply, "WSI." Opening it nervously, I peeked into a huge room full of desks. Typewriters were clacking, computers beeping, and telephones ringing. A tall, pretty woman walked up with a smile.

"Eric Sterling?" she said.

"Yes, ma'am."

"Come with me, please. Care for a doughnut?"

"Sure!"

She led me into a small room where boxes of pastries sat on a table and the smell of coffee filled the air. From a refrigerator she fetched me a carton of cold milk.

"Wait here," she said. "And eat all you want."

Boy! I dove into the doughnuts, especially the chocolate-covered ones.

Soon the lady appeared again. "Mr. Colson will see you now," she said, and giggled when she saw my face. She wiped my cheeks with a napkin, then led me down a long, wide, wood-paneled hall to a big wooden door. A nameplate said, "Mr. Colson, Director." The lady pushed the door open. The office was huge but grim, with no windows or plants or anything soft and homey. Mr. Colson sat behind a desk, looking as stern as ever.

He glanced up with a frown. "Ah, yes, Eric Sterling. Sit down. That will be all, Miss Spice."

She winked at me and left.

"Are you ready for your first assignment, young man?" Mr. Colson asked. He wore another dark suit, which made his face look very white. I could almost see the shape of his skull under his balding head. With his long, narrow nose he reminded me of an evil fox.

"Well actually, sir, there's something I need to tell you," I began.

"Oh?" His frown deepened.

"Well, you see, sir, I think there's been a mistake."

"We never make mistakes," he hissed.

"But, uh—I mean, well, the thing is, there's *another* Eric Sterling, only he spells his name differently, and I think he's the one you want for your secret agent, sir. You see—"

Mr. Colson shook his head. "Perhaps you didn't hear me, Mr. Eric Sterling. I said we never make mistakes. Can you repeat that?"

"Er, repeat what, sir?"

"We never make mistakes," he said. "Say it!"

"Uh, we never make mistakes."

"Exactly—and don't forget it. Our computer

picked *you*. It does not make mistakes. *We* do not make mistakes. Is that clear?"

"Yes sir, but—"

"Now, even if there *is* another boy named Eric Sterling—which I doubt—I'm sure he is not spy material. *You* are our agent now, like it or not."

"Yes sir, but—"

"Now! We have work to do."

I wanted to be brave and handle this like a man, but my eyes filled with tears even though I tried to hold them back. "But Mr. Colson, please, if you'll just listen—"

Mr. Colson pressed his intercom button. "Miss Spice, please bring in that case file."

"Yes, Mr. Colson," her voice piped through the desk speaker.

"Were you saying something, Eric?" he asked me.

"I was saying—"

Just then the door opened and Miss Spice came in with some papers, laying them on the desk. She smiled at me and left.

"Mr. Colson, *I am not the right Eric Sterling!*" I blurted.

He rolled his eyes, sighed, and shook his head. "All right, Eric, just to humor you, I will look one more time at your file." He pulled a folder from his desk drawer. "Now, what is your name?"

"Eric Sterling, sir. But—"

"And your parents' names?"

"Merry and Rob. But—"

He slammed the folder shut. "Case closed. You are the right Eric Sterling." He stared at me so sternly that I didn't dare open my mouth again. "Now, let's get down to business." Mr. Colson turned to the papers Miss Spice had brought. "What do you know about monitor lizards?"

I thought quickly. "Well, I've got a lizard that lives outside my windowsill. He pooches out his neck sometimes and it turns red—"

Mr. Colson cut me off with a wave of his hand. "Monitor lizards grow as big as you, boy—and even bigger," he said. "They're scattered here and there on islands in the South Pacific. Actually, they're pretty harmless when left alone—steal the occasional chicken, that sort of thing. But we believe a gang of renegade scientists is tampering with the genes of a particular species."

"Huh?"

He shook his head as if disgusted by my ignorance. "They want to change the genes of the lizard, turning it into a mutant, a giant—a sort of four-legged Frankenstein. Frankenlizard, I like to call it." He chuckled sourly.

But I didn't think it was funny. Giant lizards! "How big is 'giant'? I mean, will it be ten feet long?"

He shook his head. "Bigger."

"Fifteen feet?"

"We think they're trying to breed lizards in the twenty-five to thirty-foot range, or even bigger."

My eyes popped open wide. *A thirty-foot lizard?* That wouldn't be a lizard; it would be a dragon! It could *eat* you! "Why would they *do* that?" I asked.

His eyes narrowed. "If I knew that, it wouldn't be a mystery, now would it?" Rising, Mr. Colson pulled down a big wall map of the world and pointed to a cluster of dots in the wide blue sea. "Mariana Islands. American possession. This island here is called Baru." He tapped the map with a finger. "There's nothing there except primitive tribesmen, jungle, and wild animals. No one ever goes there—except these scientists." He sat back down.

"So what am I supposed to do?" I asked. Maybe he wanted me to write a research paper on monitor lizards so his agents would have some background.

"The day after tomorrow, you leave for Baru."

"*What?*"

He smiled coldly. "You will fly to Guam. There a yacht will take you near the island and put you in a rubber raft. When you float ashore, they will think you are a shipwreck survivor."

"But—"

"The scientists will take you in. They may be criminals, but who wouldn't help a boy lost at sea? While you're in their headquarters you will observe carefully. And if you can get your hands on some of their secret files, all the better. You won't have long, because I'm sure the scientists will contact the authorities and have you sent home. But what I want is evidence so we can make our arrests later. Any questions?"

"Mr. Colson, this is impossible! I can't—"

"I suggest you get your bags packed. I will be over this evening to talk to your parents." He snickered through his nose. "Now, be on your way. My driver will be by to pick you up at eight sharp day after tomorrow."

He steered me to the office door, his hand on my shoulder. As it slammed behind me, I felt dizzy and confused. This couldn't be happening! Me, going to a Pacific island? Giant lizards? Mad scientists?

As hard as I was trying not to, I burst into tears.

7

Something soft touched my face, and my eyes jerked open in surprise. It was Miss Spice, kneeling in front of me, dabbing my cheeks with a tissue.

"Poor Eric," she said softly. "What's the matter?"

If this wasn't the most embarrassing moment of my life, it had to be close. I mean, here I was, practically a teenager, crying like a baby in front of a beautiful woman. I tried to make some excuse for myself, but that was even worse—the words choked and wouldn't come out. I took the tissue out of her hands and covered my face with it.

"Come with me," she whispered, and led me into the doughnut room. We sat on a sofa. "Want another doughnut?"

I shook my head.

"Want to tell me about it?"

I nodded. And then, before I could stop myself, I told her everything: about the computer mix-up, and how Mr. Colson wouldn't believe me, and how I was about to be sent to certain death on a faraway island.

Miss Spice frowned. When I finished, she seemed lost in thought for a long time. Then she said, "I'll tell you what, Eric. You go ahead and get ready for your trip. I'll see what I can do." She must have seen the fear in my face, because then she smiled and said, "Don't worry. It'll be all right. I have confidence in you, even if you don't." She leaned forward and kissed my cheek.

Well, I felt a little better. At least *somebody* at WSI believed me. And Miss Spice was so nice—and pretty. She was tall and plump, with gingery hair and green eyes, and she wore a really neat orange dress. She walked me to the door, her arm around my shoulder. "Remember," she said as I left, "I have confidence in you."

That afternoon I pedaled my bike over to Bower Lane, which was less than a mile from my street. I found Sharon and Erik K. in their large backyard. Sharon sat in a wrought-iron chair at the edge of the patio, cradling a tiny monkey in her lap. On a patch of bare dirt, Erik kicked and punched a heavy bag hanging from a tree. At the back of the yard—which was surrounded by a high board fence—stood the concrete animal clinic.

"Hey, Eric C.," Sharon said. "How did it go?"

Erik K. stopped kicking and came over to listen, panting and sweaty. I told them my sad story.

"Cool!" Sharon said when I described the lizards.

Cool? Thirty-foot lizards cool? Was she crazy?

"Monitor lizards are neat creatures," she said. "Erik K., you remember when Dad brought one home from the zoo? It loved to eat out of my hand."

"Yeah, but these guys are making a *Frankenlizard*!" I protested.

She nodded. "That part's not so good. Monitor lizards can grow up to twelve feet long as it is. I'd hate to think how big they might get if a genetic scientist started engineering changes in their genes. Did Mr. Colson say *why* these scientists are doing this?"

"He said he didn't know."

I heard a lazy roar from the clinic—Leo the lion, probably—and a few other animals inside chattered and squawked in response. "Why would anybody want to create giant lizards?" Erik K. mused.

"Maybe to use in war, to attack the enemy," I guessed.

"Yeah! Wouldn't it be cool if each side had one,

and the lizards had to fight? Kind of like those old Godzilla movies!"

"That would be cruel!" Sharon protested. The monkey squirmed in her lap and crawled onto her shoulder.

"Look, you guys, this is serious," I moaned. "I'm leaving the day after tomorrow!"

"You couldn't get him to believe he had the wrong kid, huh?" Erik K. asked.

"I tried, but he wouldn't listen."

"At least that lets *me* off the hook."

"Erik K.! How rude!" Sharon chided. "Can't you see how upset Eric C. is?"

"Hey, I'm sorry," he said, punching me softly on my shoulder. "I didn't mean it that way."

"I know," I said miserably. "But what am I going to do? I'm no secret agent."

"Maybe it's not as dangerous as it sounds," Erik K. said, reaching over to tease the monkey on Sharon's shoulder with his finger.

"I sure wish we could help," Sharon said. "I'd love to see some monitors in the wild."

"I wish you could go too," I said.

"Hey, I know," Sharon said, suddenly smiling. "I don't have a monitor, but we do have a couple of iguanas. Want me to show you some stuff about them?"

"Sure, I guess."

"Yeah," Erik K. said. "And I'll show you some karate moves, just in case you have to fight your way out." He launched himself into the air and slammed his punching bag with a thundering kick. I shuddered, wondering whether I'd find myself in a situation where I had to fight like that. If I did, I was in big trouble.

"Look," Sharon said, "I've got to feed the animals. Why don't you practice with Erik K., and then we'll work with the lizards?"

I nodded, joining Erik in the yard as Sharon took her monkey and went into the clinic.

"The style I study is Tang Soo Do," Erik K. said, pronouncing it *tong sue doe*. "It's a Korean style of martial art. We mostly kick and punch."

"I noticed," I said with a sigh.

"Okay, get into a front stance, like this," he said, demonstrating.

I tried to imitate him, but I felt awkward, like I was about to fall.

"Now do your hands like this as you step forward." Erik K. showed me some kind of downward block.

Trying to step forward and move my hands at the same time was too much, I guess; I lost my balance and stumbled.

"Hmmm." He stroked his chin. "Maybe I'd just better show you some kicks. Okay, get into a fighting position, like this. That's it. Hey, that's good, Eric."

This isn't too hard. Maybe I'm starting to get the hang of it, I thought. I remembered how ferocious

Erik looked in class before he broke those boards. Squinting, I drew my lips back in a snarl.

"What's the matter?" Erik K. asked. "Got a cramp?"

I straightened up in surprise. "I was just trying to look mean."

"Oh." He pretended to cough. I didn't think it was funny. "Well, anyway, now bring your right foot up. That's the way. Whoops! Don't fall. Here, try again. Okay, right foot up, snap it out. Well, nice try, anyway. Here, do it on the punching bag. Ready? Kick!"

I slammed my foot into the heavy bag but my toes crumpled painfully. "Ee-*yow!*" I hollered, jumping up and down on one foot.

"What is it?" Sharon asked, stepping out of the clinic.

"Erik K. is trying to kill me," I said with a groan.

"I was just trying to show him a front kick," he said.

"Maybe you've showed him enough, Erik K.," Sharon said. "Come on, Eric C., let's play with these iguanas."

She went back in and returned with a pair of lizards, each about a foot and a half long. She handed me one.

"His skin feels weird. Ow! He has sharp claws," I said, as it twisted in my hand.

We stretched out on the grass and put the lizards down in front of us. "I like to get down on

their level," Sharon said. "You've got to think like they do."

"Hmmm, eye level with a lizard. Pretty strange." I didn't usually see the world like this, with my nose in the clover. From here, the iguana looked like a dinosaur. I was glad I wasn't a bug.

Sharon made a gentle hissing sound and her lizard ran over and pecked at her lips. She giggled. "You try it."

"Yuck! You think I want to be kissed by a lizard?"

Erik K., who had started hitting his bag again, laughed.

"Oh, come on, Eric C., just try it," Sharon said.

Warily, I made a hissing sound—but my iguana turned and ran away from me, seeking safety next to Sharon.

I jumped to my feet. "I'm sorry!" I said angrily. "I'm just not some superhero like you two are, all right? I knew this wouldn't work." I felt close to tears.

Sharon stood up, holding both iguanas. Erik K. grabbed me around the head. "Hey, it's okay, big guy. *I* like you," he said.

"Yeah, we both do," Sharon added. "And we're no superheroes, Eric C. We've just had some practice, that's all."

Then, to my embarrassment, for the second time today, a tear streamed its way down my cheek. Seeing it, one of the iguanas leaned forward and licked it off. Sharon giggled, and then we all started to laugh.

"See? He likes you," she said. "He wouldn't do that to just anyone."

"Yeah, and that kick—well, you almost had it; you just needed to pull your toes back," Erik K. said. "Let's try it again."

Before the day was over I had kicked the bag and kissed the lizard, and didn't feel quite as bad—that is, until I remembered my trip to Baru.

8

That night after supper, I sat in our living room with my parents and Mr. Colson, listening quietly as he told my parents that I'd been picked as a special agent for the CIA's new wildlife branch, and that it would be necessary for me to make a little trip day after tomorrow.

"But where's he going?" Mom said, obviously worried. "And what will he be doing? What about school?"

Way to go, Mom, I thought. *Hang in there.*

Mr. Colson chuckled, again reminding me of a sinister fox. "I'm afraid I can't go into detail, Mrs. Sterling. It's top-secret, and you and your husband don't have the required security clearance. But let me assure you that your son will be perfectly safe at all times. We at WSI take very good care of our agents—especially our young ones."

"I don't know about this," she said, shaking her head. "I don't like the sound of it."

Then Dad, who was managing somehow to look surprised, proud, and pleased all at the same time, leaned forward in his chair. "But, Merry, think about it objectively. This may be just what Eric needs—something to get him motivated. And he may never get another chance like this."

Fine with me, I thought.

Mom sat for a minute, nodding thoughtfully. Then she looked at me. "What do you think of all this, Eric?"

"Well—" I began.

Mr. Colson cut in. "Eric and I have talked about this at great length—after all, his feelings are important to us. I can assure you that he's very excited. Isn't that right, Eric?" He focused his fox eyes on me, and even though what I wanted to do was shout out *No!* I found myself nodding my head like a zombie. Mr. Colson continued: "Tomorrow I'll send a driver to bring Eric to the office to fill out the necessary forms before the trip. I've already spoken with his principal, who is most supportive. Eric will be allowed ample time to make up any missed schoolwork." He rose to his feet. "I'm sorry I can't say more, Mr. and Mrs. Sterling, but let me assure you that it is a great honor—a *very* great honor—for your son to be chosen." He clamped his hand on my shoulder and squeezed sharply. "I have a good feeling about this boy. He will be well taken care of." He handed my mother a business card as we stepped to the front door. "If you ever need me, at any hour of the day or night, don't hesitate to call."

"Well—" my mother said, still hesitant.

Dad shook Mr. Colson's hand. "Thank you, Mr. Colson. I'm sure Eric will make all of us proud of him."

That's *it*? You mean they're going to let Mr. Colson get away with this? But I don't *want* to go! Don't they know that?

Mr. Colson shook my hand with his dead-fish grip. "I'll see you in the morning, young man," he said. "Good night, everyone."

Two days later, I found myself staring out the window of a jet at tall stacks of white clouds in a pure blue sky. The view was exciting, but I would have liked it much better if I'd had someone to enjoy it with—my friends, my parents, maybe Miss Spice.

At the office the day before, she had pulled me aside briefly. "Don't worry—I'm working on something," she had whispered. "You just go ahead like everything is normal, okay?"

But here I was, flying to my assignment all by myself, so I guessed she hadn't been able to do anything. Right up till the time I walked onto the jet, I'd been hoping she'd get me out of this mess—or at least find a way to send Sharon and Erik K. with me.

Even though the plane contained many passengers, I felt all alone.

We arrived in Hawaii at night for an hour's layover. The climate was so nice here that the airport didn't even have glass in the windows. The warm breeze smelled like flowers.

Soon I was on a plane to Guam, a small island even farther out in the Pacific Ocean, where a WSI agent would meet me—Captain Todd, who would take me on his yacht to Baru. Since it was a night flight, there wasn't anything to see. I slept most of the way.

When the plane landed, dawn was breaking over the sea, and the clouds were pink. I was groggy, tired, and still worried about what was going to happen—but excited too. After all, I *was* getting to see new places—places I had only dreamed about. I tried to look on the bright side. Maybe this assignment wouldn't be so dangerous. Maybe it would work out all right. Maybe I could even skip final exams at school!

I walked into the air-conditioned lobby, expecting Captain Todd to meet me and tell me what to do. But the crowd surged past, the area gradually emptied, and no one seemed to be looking for me. Had I done something wrong? Could he have forgotten? I felt panic creeping over me.

Better at least claim my suitcase, I thought. *That'll give me something to do, so I won't be so nervous.*

As I walked toward the conveyor belt downstairs, I saw a tall, sandy-haired man in a shabby white suit and dented yachting cap, pacing back and forth, chomping a cigar nervously. "Ah, there you are," he said in a slight British accent when he saw me. "I was beginning to think you'd missed your flight."

I'd expected a friendly face and a warm welcome from a fellow WSI agent, but the captain seemed nervous and impatient. He grabbed my suitcase and led me outside to a battered pickup truck.

Even with all my worries, I was impressed by the island morning—warm breeze, sweet-smelling flowers, plenty of sunshine. From the airport, up on a hill, I could see rooftops and palm trees leading down to the sea.

Grinding gears and muttering every time someone pulled in front of him or slowed him down, Captain Todd sped toward the docks. "We're in a bit of a hurry, lad," he explained around his stinky cigar. "I need to drop you off and get back before dark."

I got the feeling I was just a piece of cargo to him.

As we walked down the docks past huge, beautiful sailboats, I wondered which one we would take. I'd never been on a yacht. But we passed them all and approached a tiny, grubby, oil-stained tub that looked ready to sink.

"Here she is," Captain Todd said. "Come aboard, matey."

"We're going to sea in *this*?"

He scowled. "And why not? Stand back there. That's it." He untied ropes, cranked a sputtering engine, and soon we were motoring out into a calm ocean. The wind in my face was tainted with the smell of smoke from the motor. Still, I was fascinated by the flying fish leaping across the bow. Captain Todd stood in the wheelhouse behind the steering wheel, squinting.

Beside the boat, a fin emerged from the water. Dolphins—several of them! Arching out of the water and splashing back in again, they seemed to smile. I grinned and waved, and they tossed their heads.

"Why are the dolphins following us?" I asked the captain.

He grunted. "Feeding on the flying fish, probably."

Well, maybe so, but I couldn't help thinking they liked my company, too. "Any sharks out here?" I asked.

"Of course. Last weekend a fisherman pulled in a twenty-footer."

"Twenty feet!" I wondered if he was exaggerating. That was nearly as long as this boat.

We passed a few low-lying green islands in the

first couple of miles, but soon there was nothing except ocean. I lay on the deck and peered into the purplish-blue water, wondering how deep it was. Miles, probably—miles and miles and miles. . .

"Wake up, kid."

Huh? I sat up and rubbed my eyes.

Captain Todd was squatting beside me. "There she blows."

He pointed to a long green shore not far away, lined with white beach. "That's Baru. The scientists' headquarters are straight across the island on the other side, about a mile or so. Just walk toward the setting sun. The natives live way down the island to your left. You're not likely to run into them. I'd advise you to hurry so you won't get caught out in that jungle at night." He handed me a red life vest.

"What's this?" I said. "Mr. Colson said I would float ashore in a rubber raft."

"Yes, well, my rubber raft has a hole in it. This life jacket will have to do." He slipped it over my arms and zipped it up.

"But what about those twenty-foot sharks!" I yelled.

Without answering, the tall man picked me up and tossed me over the side into the ocean!

9

I was lucky—it wasn't far to the beach, and most of the way was shallow enough to wade. Captain Todd watched until I reached shore, then he puttered away in a cloud of smoke.

The beach looked like a post-card scene: white sand, leaning palm trees, blue-green water—and nobody in sight. I felt like Robinson Crusoe.

It would have been nice just to play—build sand castles, make a fort, try to knock down some coconuts. But it was already late afternoon, and I still had to hike a mile through the jungle. I didn't like to think about what was waiting for me on the other side of the island—renegade scientists, mutant lizards. And what about the "normal" twelve-foot lizards waiting out there to ambush me? Sure, Sharon said they wouldn't bother me—easy for her to say. *I* was the one who had to face reptiles more than twice my size!

I stared at the wall of giant trees beyond the beach. I had hiked and played in woods at home, but they were nothing like this. This was rain forest! Who knew what kind of dangers lurked inside?

I said a quick prayer. My family prayed regularly at meals, of course, and at church, and I said a prayer every night in bed. But not like this. This time I really *meant* it—and I worried about whether God heard it.

Okay, jungle, here I come! I crossed the beach and pushed through a curtain of vines. It was like stepping into a different world. Huge trees rose around me, their tops blocking out most of the sky. Vines dangled everywhere.

The ground was squishy underfoot as I walked. The air hummed with insects. *Screech!* A bird shot out of a bush close by, and I jumped. I sank to my ankles in mud—yuck! And it sucked at my feet as I tried to pull them out.

I slogged on. A spider web clogged my hair. Mosquitoes sang in my ears. Branches poked my face and grabbed at my wet clothes. When I heard my heart beating fast and loud in my ears, I realized I was getting panicky. The forest seemed to be choking me, strangling me, dragging me down. . .

"No!" I shouted and leaped blindly forward—only to trip on a vine and flop face-down in the muck. I scrambled up and sprinted, not caring which direction I ran, wanting only one thing—to get out of that jungle that was closing me in. Sweat poured down my face; I used my arms like machetes, hacking vines and branches aside—and suddenly the ground dropped away and I landed neck-deep in a narrow, overgrown creek. Stifling a scream and thinking of pythons, I clawed my way up the far bank, driving dirt painfully under my fingernails, and plunged into the jungle again through a thicket of thorns that ripped my clothes and skin.

Suddenly I burst through a wall of leaves and found myself on a well-trodden footpath. Bright blue butterflies danced in rays of golden sunlight. Birds tittered happily. I leaned against a tree to catch my breath.

I had made it. I had survived the jungle. Still panting, I glanced down and saw how filthy I was. An embarrassed grin spread over my face. Man, had I ever panicked! Pretty silly. Nothing had hurt me; nothing was out to get me. And now here I was safe and sound in the sunlight again. "Just walk toward the setting sun," Captain Todd had said. All I had to do was follow this trail.

I washed off at the little brook I had crashed through, then set off down the path. Just being on a clear, open trail made me feel safer, maybe because I could see a little way ahead.

The scientists wouldn't have any problem believing I was a lost shipwreck survivor—I was dripping wet and wearing a life vest. All I had to do was watch what the scientists did while I waited for a rescue ship to come, and then go back home and tell Mr. Colson what I'd seen. Nothing to it! Maybe I could even go home as early as tomorrow!

Now that I had a clear path to follow, I was making great time. I would be there before long. A mile wasn't so far, really. I walked to the mall sometimes, and it was about a mile. Maybe the scientists would have supper ready. I hadn't eaten lunch, and boy was I hungry!

The path entered a dense thicket of tall, green stalks I recognized as bamboo, but this was definitely the biggest bamboo I'd ever seen—the stalks were three or four inches across. The thicket closed around the path so that I couldn't see ahead. Then, rounding a curve, I froze. There on the path ahead of me was a boy holding a machete, staring straight at me.

The bamboo thicket rustled, and I found myself surrounded by a gang of island boys about my age or a little older.

When Mr. Colson had said tribesmen, and Captain Todd had said natives, I had pictured people wearing almost nothing but bones in their noses and paint on their faces. These kids were brown-skinned and black-haired, but in dress they were totally different from my mental picture. They wore shorts and T-shirts with logos like "Live and Die in L.A." and "M.C. Hammer."

"Uh—hi," I said, trying not to sound frightened. "I'm Eric Sterling, and I'm trying to get to the scientists' headquarters." *Oops—hey, good job, secret agent,* I thought. *You're supposed to be a shipwreck survivor. You're not even supposed to know there are scientists here.*

The boy in front of me scowled and stepped forward. I kept my eye on his machete and tried to step back, but there were other boys behind me.

"You makim what?" he said.

"What?"

"What you doin' here?" This guy had the weirdest accent I'd ever heard. He was speaking English, all right, but I could hardly understand him.

"Well, I just washed ashore, and—"

"What we fellas gon' do wit' him, Bimmu?" asked one of the boys.

Bimmu—that must be the name of the tall guy in front of me. He was lean and muscular and wore a shirt that said "Bad Company." He sneered. "Come, we takim 'im to treehouse. This-fella boy he belong us, now."

10

To say that my first secret mission for WSI had taken a wrong turn would be putting it mildly. I'd been captured by machete-wielding natives who could barely speak English! My hope for a hot supper and a flight home tomorrow faded; I just hoped I'd be *alive* tomorrow!

They prodded me down the trail for a short distance, and then Bimmu veered off into the jungle, hacking at vines and branches with his machete. The others pushed me after him. Even with Bimmu clearing a path, walking through the dense undergrowth was hard.

At last Bimmu stopped, pointing at a nearby tree. "All right. You go up this-fella tree."

A rough, homemade wooden ladder leaned

against the trunk, leading to a bamboo treehouse I could barely see among the leaves high overhead.

"Quick-time!"

I scampered up the ladder and climbed into the treehouse through a trapdoor in the floor. The boys came in after me. There were five of them, and Bimmu was the biggest. We all sat down.

"Now, what-for you doin' in our bush?" Bimmu demanded.

"I washed ashore after my boat sank. I didn't know you guys owned this place."

Another boy, chubby and almost friendly looking, spoke up. "We fellas don't own it. We just like play here, that's all."

"Fasten mouth, Moki!" Bimmu ordered. "This bush belong us! We no like outlanders."

"Where are your parents?" I asked.

"Yes," Moki said. "Sun he going down, Bimmu. You-me-fellas must go to village or parents killim us."

The other boys chuckled and nodded.

"Moki, I said fasten mouth!" Bimmu said. "True, we got parents. They no got sense. By and by we grow up big-fellas and makim what we like all-time."

I didn't understand half of what they said, but it really didn't matter, because there was only one thing I wanted to know. "What are you going to do with me?" I asked.

"You belong me-fellas. You outlander," Bimmu said contemptuously.

I'd just known that something like this was going to happen, no matter how many times Mr. Colson told me this assignment would be easy. Sure. Easy for him. *What would a real secret agent do right now*, I wondered, trying to remember movies I'd seen. I decided to try a bluff. "Look, I've got to get to the scientists' headquarters tonight—or they'll come looking for me."

Bimu ignored me. "You stop here tonight. In morning we think what we like makim wit' you. No-good you try run away. We movim ladder."

The other boys seemed anxious to get home; they rose to go.

"Hey," I said, "I haven't eaten all day. Can't you at least give me something to eat and drink?"

"No, outlander!" Bimmu sneered as he followed his friends down the ladder. "We no give you nothing."

I watched them climb down. Then Bimmu unfastened the ladder and dropped it. The gang quickly disappeared in the dusk.

I looked around to try to find a way to escape. They'd done a good job on the one-room tree-house; it was made of poles lashed together with vines under a thatched roof. I shook the wall; it seemed solid. My tree had no lower branches, and it was too big around to shinny down. Even if I could get into one of the surrounding trees, they were pretty much the same.

A scraping sound close by made me jump. The top of the ladder appeared against the tree again, then Moki's head poked up through the trapdoor.

"Here," he said, handing me an open coconut and a clump of yellow bananas. "No good you go hungry."

"Thanks, Moki. Listen, can't you let me go? I really need to get to the scientists' headquarters. It's important."

"Why you want go there? That place no-good true."

"Because, uh—well—I can't tell you."

He scowled. "Like Bimmu say, you belong us now, outlander." He disappeared down the ladder and moved it away from the tree again.

I drank thirstily from the coconut, which tasted like bubbly sweet water. Then I began greedily eating bananas. I ate half a dozen and decided to save the rest for later.

Meanwhile, the forest got dark and hummed louder than ever with the sounds of insects and weird night creatures. At least I was safe up here—or was I? Could snakes climb trees? What other sorts of animals lived here?

I shivered and curled up in a corner of the dark hut. Closing my eyes, I started to pray silently, but I was interrupted by a deep groaning sound followed by a hiss. I peeked out the treehouse's window but couldn't see a thing. Then I heard a rustle of leaves just below my tree. Something was prowling around down there.

It hissed again, and this time I recognized the sound—lizards!

11

I was so worried about what was going to happen to me that I didn't think I'd sleep at all that night. But I did, using my life vest as a pillow. And when I woke up in the morning, the jungle glowed with golden sunlight slanting through the green leaves. The air felt hot already, but up here a gentle breeze ruffled the branches. I finished off the bananas and coconut juice, then started looking for a way down.

It didn't take long. The solution was right under my nose. This treehouse was put together not with nails, but with vines. All I had to do was pull some loose, tie the pieces together to form a long rope, and let myself down the tree!

I pulled out my pocket knife. The little blade was

dull, but it would cut through vine. I sawed a piece in two and began sliding it out from among the poles. Soon I had four pieces, each about six feet long. I tied them together, then opened the trapdoor in the floor. Knotting one end to the house, I let the other end fall. It just touched the ground. It should work—if it didn't break.

I grabbed the vine and slowly let myself down. It held, all right—tough as leather. Even so, I was plenty relieved when I finally stood on the jungle floor. Now I had to get to the scientists' headquarters quickly, before the gang returned.

Just then I heard a sound. Footsteps! And they were coming this way. Afraid of being captured again, I darted down the path in the opposite direction. After I'd run thirty or forty yards, I stopped to listen. It sounded like someone was chasing me! I couldn't stay on the path, or they'd catch me for sure. I leaped into the jungle, puffing and panting as I raced through bushes and vines, among giant tree trunks.

Suddenly a cliff wall loomed dead ahead. I was trapped! My only hope was to hide in the bushes at the base of the cliff. I crawled in on my hands and knees and lay flat.

Sure enough, the footsteps were still coming, and now I heard voices, too. I recognized Bimmu's voice, and Moki's. What would they do to me?

The breeze blowing over me here was cold, not cool and pleasant as the breeze had been when I woke up. Then I noticed that the cold breeze was blowing only close to the ground, and it was coming from the cliff. That seemed odd. Poking among the rocks at the base of the wall, I spotted a hole. Maybe it was a cave! Moving rocks quickly and as quietly as I could, I uncovered an opening big enough to wriggle into.

When I had crawled just a few feet, the hole opened up, big enough to stand up in. They would never find me now.

Almost no light came in through the small hole, so I picked my way carefully in the cool, clammy darkness. I could hear a faint sound up ahead. A waterfall, I thought. I didn't want to go far—just far enough to be safe from the boys. Just one more step should do it—

And then I was falling, sliding, tumbling feet-first down a steep, slippery slope. And just when it seemed to be leveling off and I was slowing down a bit, the bottom dropped out and my legs went over into nothing. I scrabbled with my hands for something to hang onto to keep from going completely over the edge, but my waist went over, then my chest, and just as the rest of me followed, my fingers got enough of a grip on the ledge to hold me there.

"Help!" I shouted. Even the gang would be better than this. "Help!"

My voice echoed like a thousand hungry monsters. The sound of the water was loud now, and right below me. I tried to pull myself up but the rock was too slick. My fingers were slipping—slipping—and I lost my grip.

"Aaaaaaahhhhhhhh!"

Icy black water swallowed me as I splashed into a violent underground river. I thrashed, trying to swim, but the current was too strong. It carried me along like a roller coaster.

When I heard an even louder roar up ahead, instinct made me take a deep breath. Then the current yanked me under, into a tunnel. There was nowhere to surface, no way to get air. In moments I would be dead!

Suddenly the river spewed me out into open space. I caught a deep breath as I fell, and landed *splash!* in an underground lake. The water was still cold, but at least there was no current. I floated in the darkness, treading water, listening to the gush of the waterfall.

Gradually, I began to see shapes. There had to be light coming from somewhere. As my eyes adjusted, I realized that the dim light came from beneath me. The water itself had a slight glow.

But where was the light coming from? Scuba divers with lights, coming to rescue me? Not likely. Maybe some sort of weird, glow-in-the-dark cave fish.

Then the most likely possibility occurred to me: an underwater tunnel, leading out. To escape, I would have to dive, find the hole the light was coming from, enter it, and swim toward the light until I was free.

But what if the tunnel was too long? What if I couldn't hold my breath long enough to get through it?

I would drown.

Stay in the cave until I died of hunger, or swim into a tunnel and risk drowning.

Ain't it great to be a secret agent?

12

I had never felt so scared, so cold, or so small. I knew I had to do something, and quick—the water was so icy I wouldn't be able to swim in it long. I would have to try swimming out while I still had strength.

But what if the way out was too long, or too narrow? What if I couldn't make it? I didn't want to die!

I felt panic creeping in again, and I knew I had to fight it. I closed my eyes and tried to picture some peaceful scene back home, like Mrs. Poodlum's classroom. School didn't seem so bad compared to this!

Might as well get it over with. I took a deep breath and plunged under.

I had to fight hard to swim down because of my clothes—especially my shoes. But I could see that the glow came from about ten feet below the surface, across the pool from me. My ears hurt as I swam toward it, and I held my nose and blew hard to try to equalize the pressure, the way my swimming teacher at camp had taught me. Only when I was a few feet away could I see a tunnel, just big enough to swim through, leading toward a dim source of blue light.

I returned to the surface, gasping and blowing. I knew now where I had to go and what I had to do. *Don't think about dying*, I told myself. *Think about succeeding!*

I inhaled deeply and dove again. This time I swam fast toward the tunnel, equalizing the pressure in my eardrums without slowing. Speed was the key! When I reached the tunnel, I pulled myself inside.

There wasn't much light. What if the tunnel narrowed to just a small hole, not big enough to get through?

No! Don't think about that, I told myself, *or you'll panic*.

I pulled myself along hurriedly, my head sometimes bumping against the rocky ceiling of the tunnel. The chute curved gently to the right and grew much wider and brighter, turning the water a beautiful blue-green. Suddenly I saw a large shape, something moving, something alive—

—A shark!

It was about my size, and when it saw me it turned and swam off with a quick flick of its tail.

Strangely, I didn't panic. I realized that the brighter water and the presence of the shark meant that the sea was close. If I could hold my breath a little longer. . .

I remembered that once in school, on the playground, I'd been in a breath-holding contest. I hadn't won, of course, but I'd held my breath for a solid minute. Now I felt like I'd been underwater longer than that. My lungs burned and my head pounded as I raced along.

And then—I was out of the tunnel, into a dazzling aqua-blue world. I desperately pulled myself up and up until my head broke the surface of the sea. I blew out the old air and greedily inhaled great gulps of fresh, sweet, sea air.

And the air was warm, too. So was the water, almost like a bathtub after the cold water of the underground pool. Seagulls soared nearby, calling. I floated on my back, resting my tired muscles, kicking gently to keep the waves from pushing me toward the black, rocky cliffs. On top of the cliffs were bushy green trees, and a short distance away the cliffs ended at a white beach, just like the one where I had swum ashore.

Suddenly I remembered the shark. I didn't feel so brave anymore, not out here in the open. With my last ounce of energy I zoomed to the beach, splashed ashore, and fell to my knees, exhausted—but so glad to be on solid ground, in bright sunshine, breathing fresh air.

I had escaped a hostile gang, an underground river, the threat of drowning, and a shark. And yet here I was, back where I had started, and I had to begin my mission all over again. I didn't know whether to be happy or sad.

Oh yes I did! What was I saying? I grinned. I was happy because I was still alive!

I sprawled on my back, drying off in the hot sun, eyes closed. I thought about some of the missionaries who sometimes visited our church with their stories of adventure and danger and miraculous rescues. I had often wondered what it would be like to have an adventure like that. Now I was right in the middle of one! I could just imagine myself up in front of our church someday, saying, "I was captured by bloodthirsty natives with machetes, but God saved me from the hostile natives. I was trapped in an underground tunnel, but God saved me from drowning. I swam in shark-infested waters, but God saved me from the shark."

And, to be honest, I guess he had. So far, God seemed to be taking care of me, just like those missionaries claimed he always took care of them.

As I rested, I noticed fresh footprints in the sand nearby. They looked like the marks of tennis shoes—but not *my* tennis shoes. Hmmmmm. The gang had all been barefoot. The scientists? I stood up and studied the tracks.

There were two sets, one slightly bigger than my own, the other smaller. I couldn't imagine that a grown man would have smaller feet than mine, so these probably weren't the tracks of the scientists.

And these tracks appeared to have come right out of the sea, and they led toward the jungle. Why would the scientists have walked out of the sea? It made no sense.

Warily, I began to follow.

In the rain forest, the footprints were harder to follow because of the leaves and stuff on the ground, but there were patches of mud where I could pick up the trail. They seemed to be headed toward the other side of the island, where the scientists' headquarters was supposed to be.

Wait a minute. Could it be . . . ?

No way!

But Miss Spice had said she'd try to do something . . .

The footprints came to the path, and after a few yards they were surrounded by other tracks in the mud—all barefoot.

Oh no!

I ran quickly down the trail toward the bamboo thicket, being careful not to make much noise. I slowed down and sneaked along the trail Bimmu had hacked through the thicket until I spotted the treehouse. No one was around. I placed the ladder quietly against the trunk and climbed up.

When I opened the trapdoor, there were Erik K. and Sharon—prisoners just like I had been!

13

I'd never been so happy to see anyone in my life! And I could tell by their faces they were just as happy to see me. After the hugs, we sat in a tight circle and I spluttered, "But what are you—how did you—why—"

They laughed. "Miss Spice contacted us right after you left," Sharon said. "She said she wanted us to follow you and help out if needed."

"Wow! But what did your parents say?"

"They were thrilled," she answered. "Especially Dad. He loved the idea of a special wildlife branch of the CIA. Said it's high time."

"Did Mr. Colson come talk to them?" I asked.

They glanced at each other. "Miss Spice came. She didn't tell Mr. Colson what she was doing," Erik said.

"She didn't tell him? Why not?" I asked—though I found that I really wasn't surprised. I thought I knew the answer.

"She told us how Mr. Colson wouldn't believe you about the mixed-up identity thing," Erik K. said. "She couldn't understand why he wouldn't at least check into it."

Sharon added, "So, to be on the safe side, she decided to take care of everything—sending us, I mean—by herself. Mr. Colson doesn't know."

I nodded. "So Captain Todd brought you out?"

Sharon made a face. "Yes, in that stinky tub of his."

"We had to swim ashore," Erik K. added, shaking his head. "He didn't even have any life jackets to give us."

I laughed. "I sure am glad to see you guys. But man—isn't this whole thing unreal?"

"You got that right," Erik said gloomily. "Those guys captured us before we even got started. And I've already missed one karate class."

Sharon slugged him. "Can't you forget about your karate class for once? Our lives could be in danger!"

"From who? Those punks?" He snorted.

"You saw that guy's machete," I said. "Besides, there's five of them and only three of us."

"I don't mind the numbers, but the machete is a definite problem," Erik admitted.

"Hey—we'd better go, before they come back," I said. We started down the ladder.

"What have you found out so far?" Sharon asked me.

"Not much," I answered, stepping down onto the forest floor. "I had even worse luck than you. I'll tell you about it later. My guess is if we follow that path we'll come to the scientists' headquarters. Then we can—"

"Well well, lookim this-fella no-good runaway boy," a voice said behind me.

I whirled around to see Bimmu and his pals emerge from the bushes. Sharon and Erik K. stepped off the ladder.

Bimmu appeared meaner than ever as he walked closer, clutching his machete. The others followed, looking less sure of themselves now that there were three of us. *They wouldn't be too bad if it wasn't for Bimmu*, I thought.

"All right, you-me go," Bimmu ordered.

"Where are we going?" Sharon said as she took a step.

"No more talk-talk!" Bimmu shoved her so hard she fell forward, landing on her forearms.

"Ow!"

Erik K. turned to face Bimmu. His eyes had a cold look that reminded me of the night he broke the boards.

"Why-for you waiting?" Bimmu yelled. "Walkabout now!" He raised his machete threateningly.

Then—and this happened so quickly it's hard to describe—Erik spun in a circle and slammed the bottom of his foot into Bimmu's belly, leaning away from the knife. With an "Ooof!" Bimmu staggered backward, dropping the machete to grab his stomach with both hands. Another blindingly fast kick stretched Bimmu out flat on his back, and suddenly Erik K. had one knee on Bimmu's chest, fist clenched.

The other boys had backed a short distance away, startled. Bimmu, snorting and snuffling, raised his hands. "Please! No good you hittim me again!"

For a long, terror-filled moment, I expected Erik K. to drive his fist into Bimmu's face, breaking bones as easily as he breaks boards.

Then Erik nodded slowly and got to his feet.

14

"All right. So why you fellas come this place?" Moki asked.

We all sat cross-legged in a circle. Bimmu's look of shame reminded me of a yapping yard-dog who tucks his tail between his legs and runs for his house when a doberman appears.

"What do you know about the scientists' lab?" Sharon asked.

"Place taboo. We no can go," Moki said.

"Do you know anything about the mutant lizards they're breeding?"

Moki looked confused and shook his head. "No savvy."

"Big lizards," Erik K. explained, spreading his hands wide. "Giant ones."

When the boys understood, they laughed, as if we were joking.

"This is serious!" Sharon said, then turned to Erik and me. "How can we make them understand?"

"Why make giant lizard? We thinking all scientist-man belong government," Moki said. "That why-for we no go, no ask question."

"No," Sharon said, "these scientists are not from the government. In fact, the government sent us to find out what they're doing."

"You know, I hearim big-fella roar there sometime," said another boy, "like one big-fella lizard."

Erik jumped to his feet. He wasn't, I noticed, someone who liked to sit still when there was something he needed to do. "Can you take us there?" he asked.

"Yes, but—why-for?"

Erik K. glanced at the afternoon sky. "We don't have time to explain."

To my surprise, the gang seemed to accept that and got up to leave. I guess they'd seen Erik in action, and if he didn't want to explain, that was all right with them. Soon we were all headed down the jungle path led by Moki, who carried the machete now, while Bimmu brought up the rear.

"This is so pretty out here," Sharon whispered to me as we walked. "I wish I had time to study all the animals."

I smiled. Sharon wanted to look at bugs and

monkeys, Erik wanted his karate class. My only wish was to get safely home—and soon!

Suddenly Moki stopped.

"What is it?" Sharon asked.

"Lookim," he whispered, pointing into the jungle gloom. "Lizard he go."

I got ready to run, peering into the shadows. But I could see nothing. Maybe Moki could kill it with his machete before it attacked.

"Where?" Sharon said. "I don't see it."

Moki dropped his machete, crouched, and eased forward. Then he lunged. He returned with a writhing gold-and-black lizard in his hands, maybe two feet long.

I relaxed. "Let's move on," I said, "before his mama shows up."

Moki frowned. "His mama?"

"You know. One of those twelve-footers."

He and the other boys grinned at each other; some of them laughed quietly.

"Oh yes," one of them said. "I hearim talk about lizard that big. My papa's papa talk he lookim one when he was little boy."

"But we no got big-fella lizard now," Moki told me. "Three-foot is biggest."

"Still, three feet! Won't they attack you?"

"No," Moki chuckled. "They eat rats and other little bush-fellas. And lizard he good to eat—taste like chicken." He licked his lips and grinned.

"Yuck!" I said.

"Can I see?" Sharon asked, and Moki handed her the lizard. She held it up and it stuck its forked tongue out at her.

"A monitor?" I asked.

Sharon nodded happily. This lizard definitely looked meaner than the iguana I had practiced with back at Sharon's house. The sight of it gave me goosebumps. But Sharon made a hissing sound that seemed to calm the lizard. Its eyelids slowly closed.

"Can I carry it?" she asked.

"Sure," Moki said. "We got plenty too much around here."

She perched it on her shoulder and we resumed our march, moving swiftly through the jungle. We were headed at a slight angle toward the setting sun, so I knew the laboratory couldn't be far. Sure enough, soon we spotted a sign posted on a tree: "Warning. Proceed no farther."

Moki ignored it, and we kept walking.

Another sign: "Danger. Proceed at your own risk. Place taboo."

I began to get nervous.

Then: "Extreme danger. Scientific testing in progress."

I stopped. "Wait up, you guys." They turned and stared at me. "Do you think this is safe?"

Erik snorted and started walking again, but I noticed some of the other boys seemed nervous, too.

"Come on," Sharon said to me gently, petting her lizard. "It'll be all right." We moved on up the trail, but more slowly now.

Soon we came to a huge concrete-block wall topped with barbed wire. Bright red "Danger" and "Taboo" signs were posted along it.

"Wait," Sharon said. "I want to get a look over this wall. Here, hold him, Eric C."

Before I could refuse she thrust the lizard into my hands and hurried to a nearby tree. The boys all laughed at my expression as I held it at arm's length.

"Show them the trick Sharon taught you," Erik K. said.

"No way," I said. "I'm not getting this thing anywhere close to my face."

"Go on, you big chicken," Erik scolded. "He won't hurt you. He's just a little guy."

"It's not a pet. It's wild," I answered, but, stung by the name he'd called me, I ignored my fears and brought the lizard up closer to my face, closed my eyes, and made the noise Sharon had shown me. But instead of feeling the peck of lizard lips on my own, I suddenly felt its sharp teeth closing around my nose! "Ow! Take it!" I shouted, pushing the squirming lizard to arm's length again, and scraping my nose against its teeth in the process.

Moki, laughing, grabbed it. "He no hurt you. You nose okay."

"That's how he kisses, big guy," Erik laughed.

"Well, it pinched," I pouted, rubbing my nose and looking for blood on my fingers as the boys laughed. "And I'm no chicken," I added.

Just then we heard a scream, quickly stifled. Up in the tree, Sharon was perched on a limb, peering over the wall.

We ran to the tree she was in. Clustered around the trunk, we asked, "What is it? What do you see?"

But she acted as if she didn't hear us, as if she wasn't even aware of us. "I don't believe it," she mumbled, as if she was talking to herself. "How totally—just—unbelievable!"

Erik and I started to climb after her. The other boys ran for other trees growing along side the concrete-block wall and scrambled up.

15

I'm not a great tree-climber, so it took me a little longer. I could hear the others expressing their amazement before I could climb high enough to see over the wall. Finally, I threw my leg over a branch and pulled myself up high enough to see that the wall surrounded a big dirt yard at the back of a concrete building. And right in the middle of that yard, motionless as stone, sat a huge lizard, maybe thirty feet long.

"Is it a statue?" I asked.

Just then a massive tongue slithered out of its mouth.

"Wow!" I said. "That really is—"

"Shh!" Sharon said.

The back door to the building opened and a

short, bearded man came out, holding what looked like a cattle prod in one hand and a bucket of raw meat in the other. The lizard turned slowly to face him.

"Get back, you!" the man snarled, waving the prod threateningly. With nervous, hurried movements, he dumped the meat on the ground and backed inside, slamming the door.

The giant lizard tested the meat with its tongue. Then, turning its head sideways, it took a big chunk into its mouth, raised its snout, and swallowed without chewing. I could see the bulge of the food going down its throat. The animal blinked and licked its lips. Then it took another bite. When all the meat was gone, the lizard closed its eyes contentedly.

We climbed down our trees. "What are we going to do?" I asked.

"Come," Moki said. "We-fellas must talk-talk."

We walked a short distance down the path and sat in a circle on the ground.

"How they makim lizard come up so big—and why-for?" It was Bimmu who spoke, his first words since the fight. His wonder and excitement seemed to have made him forget his embarrassment.

"We don't know why," I replied. "How? Genetic engineering."

"Gene—what?" Moki asked.

"It's too complicated to explain now," Sharon said.

"I think we must killim," Bimmu said.

"*What?*" Sharon stared in shock. "We can't kill that beautiful creature!"

"Bimmu talk true, S'aron," Moki said. "If this-fella lizard run away, he can eatim all people on island."

The other boys nodded. Even Erik looked undecided—and, to be honest, there didn't seem to be much choice. I wasn't sure *how* we'd kill a lizard that size, but if it got loose he could be a real threat. Moki was right.

Then Sharon turned to me with a pleading look. "Eric C.? Do you think we should kill it too?"

"Well, what else *can* we do?"

"Let me talk to it first."

"Talk to lizard?" Bimmu said. "You no can talk to lizard."

"You don't know my sister," Erik K. muttered.

"Look," she said. "You don't know how you'd kill it anyway, do you?" We all looked at each other, but no one said anything. Bimmu started to, then thought better of it and settled back down. "I mean," Sharon continued, "I don't think just walking up to it with a machete would be a real good idea. So give me a chance. You've got nothing to lose. If I can't prove to all of you that I can tame that lizard, then—well—then do what you have to."

"How you prove-im?" Moki asked.

She leaped to her feet. "Just watch."

"Wait, Sharon!" Erik K. called, but before we could stop her she dashed back to the wall, scampered up a tree, and climbed out on a limb over the yard. As we raced up the trees to watch, she dropped to the ground.

"Listen," she told us in a loud whisper, "if he attacks, Erik K., you drop down and distract him."

Bimmu said, "If he come at you, S'aron, we stop him quick-time!"

Sharon nodded and turned to face the gigantic mutant monitor.

It had looked plenty big before, but it *really* seemed huge compared to Sharon. It could swallow her in two bites! In fact, it looked more like a dinosaur than a lizard.

It watched her lazily as she walked toward it. Its forked tongue slithered out and tested the air. I heard a hissing sound, then realized it came from Sharon. The lizard responded with a much louder hiss. Then Sharon made a groaning sound deep in her throat. The animal answered with a growl so deep the trees seemed to shake.

It took two quick steps toward her, and I tightened my grip on the tree branch in fear. They were just a few feet apart now—a couple more steps and that lizard could gulp her down just like it had that meat! But it lay quietly, head raised, and stared at her first with one eye, then the other.

Sharon, continuing to hiss, stuck her hand out and edged forward. In the trees around me, Bimmu, Erik K., and the others silently moved into position to drop at a moment's notice and fight for her.

But as Sharon slowly, gently moved toward it, the lizard's eyelids seemed to droop. She combined a kind of musical groan with her hiss—I really don't know how to explain it. Must have been some kind of lizard talk she picked up. Whatever it was, it worked. The monitor lay its chin on the ground and closed its eyes. When Sharon touched its nose, it didn't even stir. She turned and gave us a grin.

I wanted to shout "All *right!*" but couldn't because the scientists might hear.

Now Sharon was stroking the huge creature's neck and back. It made a low, deep rumble that made me think of the lion's purr. She leaned over it, rubbing it like a big pet dog. Then, to everyone's surprise, she swung a leg over its back and climbed on. She waved at us and we all waved back like cowboys waving at a rodeo queen.

Finally she slid off the lizard and crossed the yard, standing under her tree. Staring up at us on the limbs several feet above her, she grinned sheepishly. "Uh, guys?" she said softly. "Anyone happen to have a ladder handy?"

16

While the rest of us kept our eyes peeled for the scientists, Moki chopped off a long limb with his machete. "This way," he whispered to Sharon, extending the limb down to her. The other boys helped him grip it as Sharon climbed swiftly up.

We walked back up the trail again and sat where we had before.

"Lookim, friends, sun he go down soon," Moki said. "I think you-fellas come to our place for night."

Erik K. shook his head. "I'd rather stay near the lab."

Sharon and I nodded. "We need to come up with a plan," I said.

"Sleep in treehouse," Bimmu offered. "I bring you food."

And soon the three of us were back in the treehouse—this time with the ladder still attached. It was late in the afternoon; the sun was far too low in the sky to penetrate the thick rain forest canopy, and the jungle was gloomy and dark. But with Erik and Sharon beside me, I didn't feel nearly as frightened as I had the day before.

After a while, Bimmu appeared with a big cloth sack. He poured it out onto the floor of the hut—bananas, green coconuts, and other luscious-looking fruits I had never seen before.

"This fella is pawpaw," he said, pronouncing it "poh-poh," pointing to a fat, oblong, orange-and-yellow fruit.

"Looks like a papaya," Erik said.

"This-fella here is star fruit," Bimmu said.

"Looks like a smooth green starfish," Sharon remarked.

"And I got tree pineapple, mango, and guava. No good you eatim plenty guava, you get belly pain." Bimmu chopped the tops off the coconuts so we could drink, promised to be back bright and early, and left us with our tropical feast.

"Man, this is great!" Erik said as he devoured a slice of papaya, his mouth smeared with juice.

"Whew, this star fruit is tart!" Sharon said, making a face.

"I think my favorite is the guava," I decided after I had sampled everything. "It's sweet!" But I was careful not to eat too many.

Finally we sat back, full. It was dark, but moonlight filtering through the trees allowed us to see each other dimly.

"All right," Erik said at last. "What's the plan?"

"Why not just do what Mr. Colson said—play like shipwreck survivors and get the scientists to take us in?" I asked.

"That might have worked with just one person, but I think they'd be suspicious of three, don't you?" Sharon said.

"Besides, Sharon and I didn't talk to Mr. Colson, so we can play this any way we want," Erik K. said. "Plus, his way would take too much time. Might be days before we could get the plans."

"Get the plans—that's our main objective, isn't it?" Sharon said thoughtfully.

"Well, nobody's going to believe us," I said, "But if we can get the actual papers for evidence. . ."

"Hey, I know!" Erik K. said. "What if we get the gang to create a diversion? Then one of us could sneak inside and go through their papers."

"Sounds risky," I said. "Do you know how many scientists there are?"

"Miss Spice said she thought there were two who stay here and others who come and go," Sharon said.

"Listen, this could work," Erik K. continued, getting more excited about his plan. "The gang could make some kind of racket out front. Sharon, you could be waiting in back, and sneak inside."

"What about the lizard?" she asked. "What will we do with it?"

"Ah, we'll worry about that later," her brother said, waving her concern away.

"Hey, *I'm* worried about the lizard, too," I said. "That thing can snap Sharon in two if it wants to. We got a lot of details to work out yet."

"Well," Sharon said, "we've got all night."

In the morning, Bimmu and Moki and the rest showed up bright and early. They brought us more fruit, along with some cooked meat and sweet potatoes. I tore into it like I hadn't eaten in a week. After all, I hadn't had a hot meal in a while.

"Okay, what we makim now?" Moki asked.

We told them the details of the plan we'd worked out the night before, and all except Bimmu left to go back to the village to get ready. Sharon and Erik and I went on ahead with Bimmu to the scientists' compound.

Sharon climbed a tree by the wall, ready to drop into the yard at a moment's notice. Bimmu and Erik K. disappeared around the corner of the wall, while I waited for the other boys.

Soon they arrived—and even though I'd known what to expect, the sight of them scared me. Instead of wearing T-shirts and shorts, they were dressed like savage warriors, with loincloths, feathers in their hair, cane armbands, necklaces made of teeth and claws, paint on their faces, and spears in their hands. I knew it was just stuff they had borrowed from their grandparents, but—wow!

Silently, slipping from bush to bush, we crept around the compound to the front. Then the boys lined up in front of the lab while I watched from behind a tree. At a signal from me, Moki picked up a stone and threw it at the door. It bounced off with a clang.

No response.

He threw another.

This time the door opened slightly and the bearded man peered out. The boys immediately began to shake their spears and shout their war whoops.

The man slammed the door.

Uh-oh. What if they stayed inside? Our whole plan depended on them coming out to chase us so Sharon could slip into the lab from the back.

But no, the door opened again and two men—the bearded guy and a tall, blond man with wire-rimmed glasses—darted out. Oh, *great*! They were carrying rifles! I just *knew* this plan was too dangerous!

The boys turned to run, but they were twenty yards from cover, and the men were already raising their guns!

17

Just as the men were settling their rifles against their shoulders, Bimmu and Erik K. swung into action. They'd been crouching on the roof just above the front door, and their job was to keep the rest of the boys from getting hurt. They leaped— and landed on the two scientists. The guns thudded to the ground as the four went down in a heap, wrestling madly.

Normally, I wouldn't have expected two boys my age to fare very well in a wrestling match with two grown men. But in this case, one of the boys was Erik K.—and besides, the two men were about to be outnumbered. The rest of the gang raced over with vine ropes, and in no time the two scientists were bound hand and foot. Bimmu made a loud bird call—Sharon's signal to go in the back and search for papers.

The researchers, tightly bound and sitting on the ground, looked like they were about to explode with anger.

"You stupid kids!" said the bearded man. "What do you think you're doing?"

"Outlander!" Bimmu retorted. "Why-for you makim big-fella lizard?"

"I don't know what you're talking about!" he yelled, struggling against the vines. "But I can tell you this—if you don't let us go right now, you're going to regret it!"

Erik K. walked over to me and stood with his back to the men. "Uh, Eric," he said quietly, "what *are* we going to do with these guys?"

I shrugged. "Hadn't thought about it." It was true. We'd been so busy planning everything else that we hadn't thought about what we'd do if our plan actually worked and we captured the scientists!

Suddenly we heard a shriek from inside the lab.

"It's Sharon! Come on!" Erik cried.

My first thought was, *Oh, no! There was somebody else inside the lab! Sharon's been captured!* I chased after Erik, who burst through the front door, raced toward the back, and disappeared through a door marked "Laboratory." When I caught up to him, I was sure glad to see that there was no one else in there with Sharon. She stood with her mouth

open, staring at a sheet of paper she held in her hand. "Look," she said.

Her brother took the paper and read aloud. "Men, I recruited the kid. He was suspicious at first. But he's perfect—he'll never figure out that we're just using him as a dupe. When he gets there tomorrow, make sure he gets the phony set of plans. I can use them as evidence that nothing illegal is going on there. Maybe that will take the heat off and we can get on with business."

It was signed with the letter "C."

"Colson!" I gasped.

"Here are the phony plans," Sharon said, handing me a thick file. "And these must be the real ones," she added, picking up a fat three-ring binder from the table.

I glanced at the papers. They were too complicated for me to read—lots of big words and numbers—but it didn't matter. They were evidence.

I set the file back down on the table, trying not to hear the words that rang in my ears from Mr. Colson's memo: *He's perfect—he'll never figure out that we're just using him as a dupe.* So it hadn't been a mistake after all. It wasn't Erik K. he had wanted. It was me. The guy who was too weak, too scared, and too dumb to figure out what Mr. Colson was up to. The guy who would blow the job and let Colson and his buddies keep on with whatever it was they were doing with these lizards. The perfect screw-up. Me.

"This is quite a lab," Erik said. The room was lined with stainless-steel counters holding racks of empty test tubes, jugs of chemicals, microscopes, and other items. Erik K. opened a refrigerator door; inside, there were rows of beakers containing colored liquids.

I tried to pay attention to Erik and Sharon, so that I could forget about the memo.

"This must be where they live," Sharon said, peering through a doorway that led down a hall. "Here are bedrooms, a bathroom, and—what's this?" She opened another door that led to a small, dark, foul-smelling room. I peeked inside as she turned on the light. "Chickens!" she said.

About a dozen caged chickens glared at us, as if we had interrupted their nap.

"They probably feed the lizard with them," I said.

"Hey, here's a radio," Erik called from down the hall. "Maybe one of the guys will know how to operate it, so we can call Captain Todd."

"Let's go ask," I said, and the three of us went back outside where the gang stood guard over the captive scientists.

"You guys know how to work a radio?" Erik asked. "We need to call the main island."

But before they could answer, we heard a crash from inside the lab.

Sharon ran a few steps toward the building, then stopped and turned back toward us, her face pale. "I think it's the lizard," she said quietly. "I forgot to shut the back door!"

She was right. Just then the giant head of the lizard poked out the front door and stared at us. As its tongue slithered in and out, the creature no longer appeared peaceful and contented, as it had yesterday when Sharon was stroking it. *Has it eaten today?* I wondered.

"Run!" Bimmu shouted.

"Wait!" Sharon said. "Don't run or it may attack!"

Everybody froze.

"Grab that gun," said the bearded scientist, quietly but urgently. "Shoot it before it kills us all."

Slowly, keeping one eye on the lizard, Bimmu picked up the rifle.

"No!" Sharon said. "Let me talk to it first."

She put her hand out and inched toward the monster. As soon as she began to move, it opened its eyes wider and darted forward. Bimmu raised the rifle, aimed, and his finger tightened on the trigger.

18

Moving faster than I ever remembered moving before, I slashed out at the barrel of Bimmu's gun and hit it with the heel of my hand just as the gun went off. The bullet smashed harmlessly into the ground in front of the building.

Bimmu whirled angrily. "Why you do that?" he hissed.

My hand tingled where I'd hit the metal barrel. Why? I wasn't sure I could put it into words; it had happened too fast to think about. But I pointed toward Sharon and the lizard. The huge monitor was nuzzling her neck with its nose, and she was giggling.

I'd seen something in its expression, in the way it moved, that told me that it recognized Sharon and was rushing toward her to greet her, not to eat her. Still, a quick shiver ran through me; what if I'd been wrong?

"Thank you, Eric C.," Sharon said.

"Are you crazy, girl?" sputtered the blond scientist. "That thing will eat you alive!"

"This little old thing?" Sharon said. "Why, I've seen poodles meaner than this guy."

"No good it go walkabout on island," Moki said. "Suppose it come up hungry? It can eatim people."

Sharon looked thoughtful. "It could, I suppose. Well, reptiles don't normally eat every day, so I think we're safe for now. But we have to come up with a plan. I'll lead him back to his pen. Come on, Frank."

"Frank?" Erik K. said with an amused frown.

"For Frankenlizard," I guessed, and Sharon grinned.

"We do what with these outlanders?" Moki asked, pointing to the scientists.

"Take 'em to treehouse," Bimmu declared.

"Moki, can you radio Captain Todd?" I asked. "I try."

As Sharon put Frankenlizard back into his yard, Moki called the Coast Guard on the radio in the lab and asked them to furnish the numbers of Todd's radio. Soon the captain's voice came over the radio, sleepily, as if we had wakened him.

"Captain, this is Eric C. Sterling, WSI," I said into the microphone. "I need you to come get us."

There was a long pause, then Captain Todd said, "Say 'over.'"

"What?"

"Say 'over' when you're done talking. Then I know it's my turn. Over."

"Come get us right away, please. Over," I said.

"Can't. Over," he replied.

Sharon, who had returned from the backyard, giggled.

"'Can't'? What do you mean? Over."

"Motor's broke down. Be tomorrow before I can get it fixed. Over."

"Well, come as soon as you can, please," I said. "It's important. Over."

"Ten-four. I'll be there tomorrow afternoon if nothing goes wrong. Over."

"Over and out," I said.

I was just handing the mike back to Moki when the radio's speaker crackled again and Captain Todd's voice said, "You've been watching too many of those silly old war movies. You don't say 'Over and out.' Over."

"What? Over," I said.

"When you're all done talking, you say, 'Out,' not 'Over and out.' Over.'

"Why not? Over."

"Because when you say, 'Over,' you're telling me it's my turn to talk. And when you say 'Out,'

106

you're telling me you're going to shut off your set. So saying "Over and out' is like saying, 'You can talk if you want to, but I'm not going to listen.' Over."

Moki stifled a laugh with his hand. I just rolled my eyes. "Out," I said, and hung up the microphone.

We went back outside. Bimmu, Erik K., and the other boys had left with the prisoners. Sharon, Moki, and I sat down on the ground in the warm sunshine, worn out after all the excitement.

"Moki, are there any other islands close by?" Sharon asked.

"Sure. Plenty."

"Islands with no people? Where no one ever goes?"

He thought. "Yes, we got one island, it mostly rock. Only bird go there. No people, no nothing."

"How far?"

"Oh, 'bout one mile." He pointed to the west. "Why-for you askim?"

"One more question. Do you guys have a boat?"

"Plenty. We all got canoe, for fishing."

Sharon nodded thoughtfully just as the boys returned. "We got them locked up in the tree-house," Erik K. said.

"Yes, they no run away," Bimmu added.

Unless they happen to have a pocketknife, I thought, but what I said was, "I think Sharon's cooking up a plan."

She smiled. "How soon can you get your canoes and be back here?" she asked the gang.

"We can gettim quick-time," Bimmu said.

"Where's the nearest beach?" she asked.

He pointed down a trail leading through the forest. "Close-to true."

"If you guys go get your boats and some rope, we'll be waiting for you on the beach."

"But what is plan?" Bimmu asked.

"No use asking," Erik K. told him. "With my sister you'll never know till she's ready. Come on, I'll go with you."

The boys left, and Sharon said, "Let's go get Frank."

19

To be on the safe side, Sharon offered the lizard some meat from the scientists' freezer before we left. But he wasn't interested. I guess Sharon was right about reptiles not needing to eat every day.

Next she took a cord and tied it loosely around Frank's neck so it formed a leash.

"Come on, boy," she said, hissing gently, and led the lizard through the lab and out front.

Even though I believed now that Frank wouldn't hurt us, I kept my distance. His loose skin, yellow eyes, the slow way he breathed, the movement of his head and shoulders from side to side when it walked—all those things gave me chillbumps. Sharon was so calm, though, she might as well have been leading a pony. Then I remembered how unafraid she'd been of the lion, python, and other creatures in the clinic behind her house.

We followed a path through the woods and came to a white beach. The sea was as blue-green and clear as my dad's after-shave lotion. It looked cool and inviting. Offshore I could make out the hump of an island.

"Maybe that's the one Moki told us about," Sharon said.

"Maybe. So—want to tell me what the plan is?"

She sighed and sat down in the sand. "We've got to find a home for him, Eric C."

I sat too. "What about WSI? Don't you think they'll want him?"

"What do you think WSI will do if they get their hands on Frank?"

I shrugged. "Study him?"

"Maybe. Drug him, ship him back home to the States, keep him in a cage, run experiments. An awful life."

I nodded. "Or they might just kill him."

"Right. But we can't let him loose on Baru, either. He seems tame right now, but really he's wild. I can handle him, but other people might not be able to—especially when he's hungry."

"So you want to take him to that island," I said. "The one with no people. That's why you asked the guys to get their boats."

She nodded. A breeze ruffled her golden hair. Lulled by the sunshine, the lizard sighed and closed his eyes. I dug in the sand with my fingers, finding it cool and damp underneath.

Sharon pointed down the coast. "Is that them?"

I shielded my eyes from the bright sunlight. Three canoes cut swiftly through the still water. "That's them all right. Those aren't very big boats, either." I glanced at the huge lizard. "How are we going to put Frank in one of those?"

Sharon grinned. "Who said anything about putting him in a boat?" She jumped to her feet as our friends paddled ashore.

"Boy, that was fun!" said Erik, who was panting and sweaty from paddling. "Did you know these canoes are hollowed-out logs? They're dugouts."

"So," Moki said, eyeing Frankenlizard, "what is plan?"

Sharon explained. And the boys had the same question I did: How could we get Frank across a mile of ocean in these little boats?

Sharon smiled and patted the lizard's sleepy head. "Swim."

We all stared at the huge creature. "Swim?" someone said.

"Did you bring some rope?" Sharon asked.

Bimmu held up a long piece.

"Here," Sharon said. "Tie one end to your canoe, and I'll tie the other to Frank's neck. Come on, Frank, that's a big fella. Now, Bimmu, you and Erik K. start paddling—slowly."

They eased their boat out into the shallow water,

and the rope tightened. Sharon urged the lizard to get on his feet and move toward the water.

"He might not like to swim," she explained. "But with the canoes beside him in the water I think he'll get the idea."

"Suppose he attack canoe?" Bimmu asked nervously.

Sharon ignored him. She was wading out now with the lizard. Even though Frank was huge, his legs were short, and he soon floated.

"Hurry up," Erik K. called to his sister. "Get into the boat before we get too deep."

"I've got something better than a boat," she answered. And she climbed onto Frank's broad back.

Everyone cheered. "Ride 'im, cowgirl!" I shouted. "Woo-hoo!" I jumped into one of the canoes and we followed.

"We can take turns," Sharon called.

The lizard swam slowly, but to my surprise he acted at home in the water. And he didn't seem to mind the weight of a kid on his back. After awhile Sharon got off and let one of the boys try riding. Then another, and another, and soon—*too* soon— it was my turn.

"Come on," Sharon said. "Don't be afraid."

I shuddered. Lizard-riding had never been one of my goals in life. But I didn't want everybody to think I was scared.

Slowly I slipped over the side of the canoe— onto Frankenlizard's back!

112

20

I lay flat, terrified, hugging the lizard with my arms and legs. He was floating high enough in the water that only my feet got wet. Except for the hard muscle under his skin, Frank felt almost like a giant air mattress.

"Sit up!" Sharon coaxed from her canoe. "Grab the rope!"

I forced myself to sit upright and snatched the rope collar for balance. It was scary for a few seconds, and then I realized that I was okay. I wasn't likely to fall off, and even if I did, I'd just fall into the water. Nothing to it. As long as Frank wasn't hungry.

We were about halfway to the island, moving along in deep blue water. I thought of sharks, but then I thought, *Hey, why should I fear sharks? Frank's tougher than any old shark!*

I patted the lizard proudly. He could eat a shark in two gulps.

The sea breeze ruffled my hair. Seagulls wheeled around me. Suddenly fins broke the surface—dolphins! They made a chitter-chatter noise like laughter, tossing their heads and leaping playfully. I laughed even though no one had said anything funny, just for the sheer joy surging through me—and confidence! Boy, this was great! I felt wild and free.

"I like try him now." It was Bimmu, the only one who hadn't ridden yet.

I slid off Frank into my canoe, and Bimmu's boat pulled alongside the lizard. We all watched as Bimmu tried to work up the courage to get on.

"Come on, Bimmu!" one boy called. "Why you 'fraid?"

Others laughed. "Bimmu think lizard eat him."

Frowning, Bimmu crawled onto Frank's back. Like me, he hugged tight, afraid to sit up. But at Sharon's urging he straightened up. I could see the same wonder appear in his eyes, the excitement and joy.

"Hey, this is good-fella too much!" Bimmu said.

Suddenly, with a twist and a wild swing of his tail, Frank erupted from the water head-first, and Bimmu tumbled into the sea! The lizard's huge mouth opened, his dozens of sharp teeth glisten-

ing in the sun—and then at the peak of his leap his long tongue lashed out and snared a low-flying seagull. In seconds, the bird disappeared down Frank's throat.

"Gross!" I said.

"Man! Cool!" said another boy.

Bimmu surfaced, splashing first in one direction, then another. "Help! Help! He try'm eat me!"

We all laughed, and Bimmu realized he was safe.

"He hungry all right, but he think bird taste more better than you, Bimmu," Moki teased.

"Hey, Sharon," I said, a thought just occurring to me. "I thought he wasn't hungry."

She shrugged. "I guess he couldn't resist," she said, brushing back her damp hair.

"Maybe he no can resist you too, Bimmu," one of the boys giggled.

I'm sure he'd have rather climbed back into the canoe, but Bimmu's ego had taken enough beating. Nervously, he pulled himself back onto the big lizard, who now looked sleepy and content.

"Well," I said to Sharon, "Frank sure won't have any trouble catching his own food, will he?"

She smiled. "Lizards are great hunters."

As we neared the island, I could see that, unlike Baru, it was rocky and barren. Higher up, thousands of birds roosted.

On shore, Sharon unfastened Frank's rope. Then she hugged his broad neck.

"We're going to miss you, big fella," she said sadly.

Frank just wagged his head sharply back and forth. Maybe he was saying goodbye, or maybe just shaking the water from his ears. Then, as Sharon backed away from him, he lifted his body out of the sand on those short, sturdy legs and moved toward higher ground.

"Bye, Frank!" we chorused.

He looked back at us once with curious, reptile eyes, then walked slowly across the beach and into a rocky canyon, his huge tail moving from side to side until it vanished.

Sharon stood with her back to us, staring after him. Her shoulders shook gently. Erik put his arm around her. "It's okay, Sis. We can come back and visit."

"No," she said, snuffling. "It's better if he doesn't have visitors. It's better if he lives his life out alone here, wild and free."

Without the giant lizard swimming behind us, our canoes moved swiftly on the way back to Baru. But instead of returning to the beach near the lab, we angled the canoes along the shore.

"We go to village," Moki explained. "We got surprise for you fellas."

Rounding a point, we saw a cove ringed with palm trees. On the beach a number of boats were moored, from dugouts to sailboats. Shiny tin roofs gleamed among the trees, as well as roofs made of

117

leaves and grass. Smoke rose from big outdoor fires surrounded by people.

As we landed, the whole village welcomed us. There must have been fifty people. The women wore loose, long, colorful dresses and the men either wrap-around skirts or pants. There were even girls our age; like the boys, they tended to dress in more modern style. The people placed flowery wreaths around our necks and greeted us with smiles and hugs.

"This is mumu," Moki explained, pointing to heaps of smoldering earth. "Food cookim all night inside hole. It come up plenty good too much! You fellas hungry?"

"Are we ever!" exclaimed Erik K.

Soon the village people removed boards and palm fronds from the heaps and pulled out bundles of food wrapped in banana leaves. As they opened them, we saw steaming piles of sweet potatoes, pork, fish, corn on the cob, greens, bananas, and kinds of food I'd never seen before. People gave us green coconuts full of juice, and we sat in the shade and stuffed ourselves. Boy, did we eat! And eat and eat! Some of the boys even took food to the captive scientists, too.

That afternoon, we borrowed swimsuits and played in the sea. Using a mask Moki loaned me, I swam in the shallows looking at the odd-shaped coral. Little fish darted here and there, their colors brighter than anything on land.

That night the village held an outdoor church service around a bonfire. Sitting next to Sharon, Erik, and the other kids, I listened to the hymns. The tunes were the same ones we sang at our church back home, but the words were different. I hummed along, but quietly, so I could listen. Other than rock, I didn't like much music—but this was beautiful! The fire popped and crackled, sending sparks shooting upward. I peered up at the stars and realized I had never seen so many. *Amazing*, I thought. *These people are so different from us. But they sit under the same sky and sing the same hymns to the same God.*

Erik nudged me. "Boy, I *like* this kind of church service!" he whispered.

Sharon nodded. "Maybe we can get our preacher to hold some kind of outdoor service," she told her brother.

At last we all turned in, the three of us sleeping in guest huts. Lying on a cane mat while the sea breeze sighed in the roof thatch, I slept better than I had in a long time.

21

In the morning some of the boys took the laboratory chickens back to the village while the rest of us took food to the two scientists, who were still sitting in the little treehouse, cramped and grumbling. I had to chuckle—they were smart enough to figure out how to breed a thirty-foot lizard, but not clever enough to escape from a treehouse I'd managed to escape from myself!

After we moved the ladder away, I pointed through the jungle. "The cave where I hid when you guys chased me is over that way," I told Moki.

"What cave?" Erik asked. "You haven't told us about that."

"I haven't had time. Come on—I'll show you."

I led the way as we all trooped single-file

through the forest. At last I spotted the cliff wall and the clump of bushes at the cave entrance. "It used to be a lot smaller," I said, getting down on my belly and poking my head into the hole. "I had to open it up some."

I crawled in, and my friends followed.

"I no savvy this-fella cave," Moki said as we stood up. His voice echoed in the dripping darkness.

"Over there is where I fell," I said. "Come take a look."

"Be careful," Sharon cautioned as she and the others slowly followed me deeper into the cave.

"Don't worry." I chuckled. " I know this cave like the back of my—" Suddenly my foot slipped on the smooth, wet stone, and the floor fell away and I dropped into the same chute as before! "—haaaaaaannnnnd!"

I tumbled into darkness, moving so quickly this time that I wasn't even able to grab the ledge. I just pitched straight out into space. Even though I knew what to expect, the icy water I plunged into shocked me to the bone. But there was no time to think; the current swept me along, I heard the roar up ahead, and I took a deep breath. The river sucked me under and through the tunnel and spewed me out into the underground lake.

"This can't be happening," I sputtered, treading water. "It can't happen twice to the same person. I must be dreaming. *Oh*, that's cold!"

But I wasn't dreaming. I was trapped in the same underground lake as before. One way out. But how could I possibly make myself swim through that long, dangerous, scary tunnel again? Once in a lifetime was enough. And suddenly I remembered the shark I'd seen in the tunnel.

I slapped the water with my hand in despair. I had come all this way, and now this!

I turned onto my back and floated, wondering what to do. As I watched, I thought I saw a chink of light open up in the cave ceiling overhead. Was it an illusion? Were my eyes playing tricks in the blackness? But it didn't disappear, and then bits of dirt sprinkled around me. I watched, confused and amazed, as the hole grew bigger. It looked as if boards were being moved away. Then I saw heads peering down, silhouetted against the sky.

"Eric C.? Are you in there?" Sharon called in a concerned voice.

"Down here!" My words echoed in the cavern.

"Just wait! Bimmu and Moki are going to get some vines to make a rope. Are you all right?"

"Yes! But I'm c-cold!"

In a few minutes the boys appeared and lowered a thick vine rope to the water. I grabbed hold and tied it around my waist. The hole was close enough to the side of the cave that I was able to "walk" up the rough wall slowly as they pulled. Finally I was able to crawl out.

"Thank goodness!" Sharon exclaimed.

"How did you find me?" I asked, shivering.

Moki grinned. "Lucky guess. I no savvy other cave, but I savvy this-fella. I think maybe they one-one."

"But how did you get out before?" Erik asked, puzzled.

With my teeth still chattering, I told them the whole story—about the underwater tunnel that led to the sea, and the shark I had surprised, and how I'd spotted tracks on the beach.

"Man, that's incredible," Erik said, punching me lightly on the shoulder. "That took guts."

"Are you kidding? I was scared to death."

"Listen!" Bimmu said, cupping a hand to an ear.

In the distance we heard the puttering of a motor.

"Captain Todd," Erik K. said.

"Come," Moki said. "We go get outlanders."

22

"Come in, come in! I'm so happy to see you!" Miss Spice greeted the three of us with hugs as soon as we came through the door back at WSI headquarters.

She led us down the hall to Mr. Colson's office—only now the nameplate on the door said "Miss Spice, Director." "Please, sit down," she said, and took her place behind the desk. A secretary brought in a platter of doughnuts and cartons of milk.

"Oh boy!" Erik K. said, grabbing a doughnut.

Miss Spice laughed. "As you can see, there have been plenty of changes around here since you left."

We nodded, chewing.

"Captain Todd faxed us the documents you found, including the letter, and Mr. Colson was promptly arrested. Of course, those two scientists were also charged, along with the others involved. I still can't get over what a fabulous job you kids did!"

I shook my head. "It was Erik K. and the boys who captured the scientists, and Sharon who tamed the lizard."

"See?" Erik K. said. "He keeps saying he didn't do anything."

"You underestimate yourself, Eric C.," Miss Spice said.

"I what?"

"If you hadn't been suspicious of Mr. Colson from the start, his plan might have worked. But as it was, you tracked down Erik K. and Sharon— and you had the good sense to confide in me."

"Let's face it," I replied. "Mr. Colson picked me on purpose because he knew I wasn't qualified. I was a 'dupe,' he said. He knew I'd blow it."

"But you *didn't* blow it," Miss Spice said.

"Only because of Erik K. and Sharon."

"Who was it that escaped from the treehouse and then came and freed Sharon and me?" Erik said.

"Yeah, but the gang showed up before we could get away," I argued, "and then it was you who beat up Bimmu."

Sharon spoke up in a soft voice. "Who was it

that stopped Bimmu from shooting the lizard, Eric C.?"

I looked at her and remembered the lizard darting toward Sharon, and Bimmu raising the gun to shoot.

"You all deserve equal credit," Miss Spice said. "You three are quite a team. I expect WSI will be calling on you for more assignments in the future."

I rolled my eyes, not sure whether that was good news or not.

"I still don't understand why they were breeding giant lizards," Erik said, studying the doughnut platter thoughtfully before selecting another.

"I think I know," Sharon said.

"You?" he said. "How could you know?"

"Remember when Moki caught that lizard in the jungle?" she asked. "Remember what he said?"

We shook our heads.

"He said they're good to eat."

"That's right!" Erik K. snapped his sugar-coated fingers. "He said they taste like chicken."

"The scientists were breeding them as a food source!" I guessed.

Sharon nodded. "When I saw the chickens at the lab, I was pretty sure. You thought the scientists were feeding the chickens to the lizard, Eric C.—but there weren't enough of them for that. So I decided that the scientists were using them in their experiments."

Miss Spice nodded. "The scientists were being paid by a large poultry company to find a cheaper source of meat. Think how many chickens it would take to add up to one thirty-foot lizard!"

"But who would eat lizard?" I said, making a face.

"I'll bet they wouldn't tell anybody it was lizard," Sharon said. "They'd probably call it 'island turkey' or something."

"Exactly right," Miss Spice said. "And that's the first law they violated. It's clear from the documents you recovered that, as we suspected, they were conspiring to defraud the public into believing that the lizard meat was actually poultry. In addition, federal laws are quite strict about genetic engineering, and so they bribed Mr. Colson to help hush it up. Conspiracy to defraud, violation of federal genetic engineering laws, bribery—I'm afraid our scientists, Mr. Colson, and some poultry company officials may draw some serious prison time."

"Boy, that's incredible!" said Erik K.

We sat and thought it over for a minute or two, and then I shook my head. "There's only one thing that bothers me," I said.

"What's that?" Miss Spice asked.

"Well, you see, we've already missed a week of school, and finals are coming up, so—uh—Miss Spice, do you think you could arrange for us to skip the exams?"

She folded her hands. "I've already talked with your teachers. They say with a little extra studying at night, all three of you will be caught up in time to take your tests."

I groaned. "Nice try," Erik K. whispered.

Later I stopped by my neighbor Harvey Blast's house. As usual, he was slouched in front of his computer, studying complicated tables. I told him the whole story.

He didn't act surprised. "Look, it's really very simple," he said. "If you start with a core of baseline information and identify the trends, you can usually predict how things will turn out. You should have just come to me, presented me with all the facts you had, and I could have computed everything."

"Really? Hmmm." I stroked my chin thoughtfully. "Let me ask you this. If I bring you all the grades I've made so far this year, can you tell me how I'm going to do in the final exams?"

Harvey grinned and turned his computer off. "I'll never tell."